Odessa

Annie Seaton

Pentecost Island 7

Be yourself. Everyone else is taken.

Oscar Wilde

Prologue

Pippa - Pentecost Island - October

The night before our wedding I moved out of Rafe's house and slept down at Aunty Vi's with Nell and Tam. Funnily enough, I still thought of the old house as Aunty Vi's, even though she had passed a couple of years ago and the 1930s house and half the island had been left to me.

Nat and Gabe, Nell and Tam's partners, had gone to Rafe's for the night, so we were indulging in a girls-only night. Like old times, if we could call a year ago, old times. We stayed up late, chatting and reminiscing. Much laughter and giggling fuelled by champagne—for Nell and I anyway—filled our night, and there was no talk about work or the resort.

'Might as well act like teenagers again for a while. You're going to be an old married woman this time tomorrow,' Nell said.

'Seriously, Pip, are you sure this is right for you? Are you happy?' Tamsin asked. Nell was usually the worrier for all of us, but Tam was drinking soda water and wasn't tiddly like Nell and I were. Since she'd become pregnant, she seemed more serious and worried more.

'I am. Absolutely, unequivocally, damn straight sure. And I'm in lurve.' I spread my arms wide and knocked Nell's shoulder. 'I wouldn't change tomorrow for the world.'

Nell nudged me in retaliation and champagne slopped out of my glass onto the threadbare, but comfy sofa.

'Woops.'

We both giggled and Tam did her famous eye roll. 'No Darren or Eric regrets?' she persisted.

'Ooh, wash your mouth out, Tamsin Jones,' I protested.

'With soda water,' Nell snorted.

'At least one of us is sober,' Tam said with a smile.

'Remember what Aunty Vi used to say to me?' I said mopping at the damp sofa. 'Positivity, Pip. Well, you know what? I'm so certain of Rafe, I don't ever need to say or think that anymore. I've found the love of my life. And I trust him implicitly. Rafe would never hurt me.' My voice softened and I gazed dreamily up to the hill where the lights of my partner's house glowed softly in the dark.

'Okay, it was just a last minute check.' Tam lifted her glass and sipped her soda water. 'I never dreamed in a million years that the resort would grow like it has. I remember when we met you in Solaris last year and you read the letter from that solicitor, Mr Morton. We imagined we'd be letting out rooms in Aunty Vi's old house to kayaking backpackers but, holy shit, girls, look at us now!' Her grin matched ours.

'We've done good,' Nell said. 'Really, really good.'

'And don't forget we've worked hard too.' I grinned at Tam. 'But it's just as well you saved Eliza from drowning. What a difference that's made to us.'

'And just as well Sienna came to visit,' Tam replied.

Nell giggled again. 'And just as well you didn't turn Evie back when you saw that pink sail.'

'I could have, couldn't I? But I've got over my pink phobia. Those days are long gone. The memories, the reminders of sad times. All gone.'

'Please don't tell us your top secret wedding dress is pink!' Nell wagged her finger at me, and I laughed when she almost slid sideways off the sofa.

'It's all right for you pair on the bubbles and giggling.' Tam yawned. 'If I drink any more soda water, I'll be up to the loo all night. I'm going to bed. I can't get over how much more sleep I need now.'

Nell hiccupped. 'Well, you're sleeping for two now.'

'Not sleeping for two, you airhead.'

Nell and I must have been tiddly to earn a second eye roll from Tam.

'That's eating for two, and boy, I'm doing that,' she said.

'Airhead?' Nell managed to sit up straight. 'I am not an airhead. I am a resort manager.'

'Hey, gals?' I pushed myself up off the sofa. 'Before you go to bed, come down to the beach with me and look at the moon. My last moonrise as a single woman.' A strange feeling fluttered through me. Maybe it was the champagne, or maybe it was the thought of the new direction my life was about to take.

Married. Who would ever have believed it?

'A group hug by moonlight,' Nell said as we left the house.

Together, we made our way carefully along the path without speaking and crossed the beach to the rock where we always sat. The full moon had risen and hung heavy above the horizon. The night sky held a tinge of pink and the brisk wind had whipped up small waves on the usually calm passage. The water held a grey and ominous look and I shivered, hoping it wasn't a premonition.

We sat quietly side-by-side on the edge of the wide flat rock as we had done many times over the past twelve months.

'Everything's changing, isn't it?' I said, with a break in my voice.

'But would you really want things to stay the same, or go back to the way it was before we came to Pentecost Island?' Nell asked.

'No, but just for one hour, I'd like to go back and see Aunty Vi in her house and tell her how it was going to be.' I swallowed the emotion. 'Tell her how happy I am, and how it was meant to be that she sold half of the island to Rafe.'

'I know she'd be happy, Pip, and that's what you have to remember and hold close in your heart,' Nell said.

I was sitting in the middle, and Tam reached over and put her arm around my shoulder, and then Nell did from the other side.

'Make me a promise, girls. No matter what happens, we're still—'

'All for one, and one for all,' we chanted together.

'I love you pair. Ever since you were kind to me at primary school. Friends for life,' I said hugging them back.

'We'll still come down here to watch the moon rise when we're old and grey,' Tam said.

'Nah.' Nell shook her head. 'We won't get our walkers over the rocks.' She snorted again and I joined in with a giggle.

'Come on, you two.' Tam stood and pulled us to our feet. 'It's time we were in bed. There's a wedding tomorrow and you need your beauty sleep.'

***

Surprisingly, I slept well. Being back in the old house with Nell and Tam had been an excellent decision for the night before my wedding. Their constant chatter and our laughter kept me calm. We had breakfast together, and then Nell asked me to keep her company in the office. Tam went across to the new kitchen to see if Angus and Cherry needed any help. There was no sign of the other girls, but each time I suggested going to find them, Nell found something to keep me occupied. I narrowed my eyes and wondered what they were up to. I knew these girls well.

The morning passed quickly and Tam prepared lunch for us. We sat on the veranda and could hear the chatter and clatter from the kitchen as the casual chefs prepared lunch for the resort guests who were seated on the side veranda. The inhouse guests would be served dinner here tonight while our wedding reception was in the new restaurant and bar.

'Cold drink? Champagne? Coffee?' Nell asked when she came out of the office.

'No champagne until we go down to Sienna and the day spa,' I said as Tam put a platter of cold meat and cheese on the table. 'I can't wait. She is so talented. I was floating when she did the practice run on Thursday.'

'Is your dress down there already?' Tam asked.

I nodded. 'Sienna and Evie had a sneak peek so they could get my makeup and hair right.'

'Ooh, I can't wait to see it,' Nell said. 'Is it a white wedding dress? Come on, give us a clue.'

'Nope. Not long to wait now.' I fanned my hand in front of my face.

'I'm getting more excited by the minute.'

'That's why I kept you busy, so the nerves couldn't kick in.'

When we'd finished lunch, Tam headed for her shower, and Nell went to tell Tess, the part-time office assistant, it was time for her to man reception.

I waited on the veranda for Tam and Nell to walk down to the day spa with me. On the way down, when we reached the small glade, I stopped, and Tam bumped into me.

'What's wrong? Nell asked. 'Did you forget something?'

'You haven't changed your mind, have you?' Tam's brow wrinkled in a frown.

'No, of course not. I just want to tell you both something I forgot to say last night. You know, me being married isn't going to change our friendship.'

'Of course it's not. And me being a mum won't either,' Tam said looking relieved.

Nell nodded slowly. 'Things will change, but one thing I do know is that our friendship is strong enough to take change.'

'Good. That's sorted then.' The soft warm breeze caressed my skin as we began walking again. It was a brilliant Whitsundays afternoon; the sky and the water were both such a deep blue you could barely see the horizon where they met. I couldn't have asked for a better day for our wedding. Serenity filled me and I let out a soft sigh.

The noise of a boat motor easing back caught my attention as we passed the beach on the way to the day spa. I turned to look at our bay. Jiminy's boat was approaching the wharf and I frowned. He and his wife, Sarah, were guests at the wedding, but they were arriving very early. The ceremony wasn't until three o'clock, and it was just past noon.

I was further surprised when Rafe hurried down the steps from his house, but I let my eyes take my fill.

He must be coming down to see why they were early, I thought.

His dark hair glinted in the midday sun as he headed towards the jetty. Even though I'd enjoyed the girls' company last night, and slept well in my old bed, I'd missed having Rafe beside me. As I woke at first light, I'd reached out for him, before I remembered where I was and that it was our wedding day.

Rafe jumped down to the wharf and ran towards the boat as Jiminy secured it. The gate at the side of the deck opened and I stared as a tall slim woman in white stepped onto the jetty. It wasn't Sarah, and to my knowledge there were no new guests arriving today. We'd cleared the bookings calendar for the wedding day. The only guests in-house were those who were already on the island.

Rafe held his arms wide open as he reached the woman.

Clutching her broad-brimmed white hat with one hand she fell into his arms and clung to him with the other. He embraced her and my fiancé's dark head rested against the woman's for a long time.

A very long time.

A moment later, an older couple stepped off the boat and joined them.

Then it hit me. These were Rafe's publisher friends and their daughter, Odessa. I thought they had cancelled because of the accident. Why hadn't Rafe told me they were coming?

'What are you looking so worried about?' Tam asked.

I pointed to the boat. 'We have unexpected guests.'

Tam peered past me. 'Who?'

'I know I'm being a bitch, but why the hell did she have to arrive today of all days? On our wedding day!'

'Who? Who is it, Pip?' Tam put her hand on my shoulder, and I took a deep breath.

'A friend of Rafe's from England. We were expecting her for a visit, but not yet. Or at least I wasn't. She's had a horrible tragedy in her life, and she was coming here in a few weeks to help her That's her parents with her. They own the company that publishes Rafe's books. He invited them to the wedding, but they had to say no, because she was still in hospital. And I didn't think she was invited.'

'Maybe they decided to come after all, and travel with her.' Tam frowned.

'But now that they're here, where will they stay?'

I shrugged and tried not to sound worried. 'I don't know. I'm right out of the English friend loop.'

'Nell, we're not full, are we?' Tam asked.

'No, but the vacant huts haven't been serviced, because the cleaners haven't come over today. I'll go and see Tess right now, and get it sorted, because they can't stay with you and Rafe tonight. It's your wedding night, for goodness sake.'

'I know,' I said glumly as Nell took off back to the office.

And more to the point, why hadn't Rafe told me she was arriving? I thought. He must have known that she, I mean, they were on the way, I told myself. All I could think of was the way that Odessa had clung to him, and he had held her close.

'If the worst comes to the worst, I'll make up your bed here with clean sheets, and Gabe and I can give up our room too, and go to a single bed for the night,' Tam said.

'Thanks, sweets, but it'll be fine. Tess has cleaned the rooms before. If she needs to, we'll pay her extra.' I forced a calm smile to my face. 'I'm really happy that Rafe has some friends here for him today too.'

'Are you ready, girls? Where's Nell hurried off to?'

I jumped. I hadn't seen Sienna coming along the path.

I turned to her as she stood beside Tam and I. 'Nell won't be long.'

Sienna took my hand. 'Hebe Day Spa awaits you. We have just over two hours to make the three of you even more beautiful. Evie's waiting down there. She's set up a mini-hair salon in the other treatment room. Are you excited, ma cherie?'

'I'm happy.' I forced myself not to look at the jetty or the group heading for the steps leading up the cliff to Rafe's house.

As I walked through the dim forest with Sienna and Tam to get ready for my wedding, my serenity was tainted by a growing doubt. My past rushed through my thoughts. I should have known that things wouldn't work out perfectly.

I also knew I shouldn't doubt Rafe because of my past. I couldn't do that.

But all I could see was him holding that woman close to him. Their heads together as though they were a couple. Was it too late to change my mind?

Chapter 1

Odessa
August -London

'Come on, Han. It won't make us too late. There's a sale on, and we could get some new dresses and shoes for the weekend. I really need a dress for your Gran's birthday tomorrow night.' Odessa Walker reached over and tugged her friend, Hannah's arm as Hannah gripped the steering wheel of the Aston Martin. 'Harrods is only a couple of blocks from where we join the motorway.'

'Careful, Essie, Daddy will kill me if I so much as put a scratch on his car.' Hannah shrugged Odessa's hand off as she focused on the road ahead. 'Driving through those narrow country lanes is enough of a worry, let alone trying to find a park in Knightsbridge.'

'You need to be a more confident driver, sweets. If you didn't worry as much about other drivers and just focused on the road and drove at a decent speed, it would be much easier. Let me drive, we'll get there faster.'

'Says the woman who lost her license for speeding last month.' Hannah chuckled as she slowed the car to a crawl as they approached the turnoff. 'Of course you're not going to drive my father's car. God in heaven, I'd be cut out of the will.'

'My father's publishing office is there, and we can park at the side. Come on, please?' Odessa was well-practised in getting her own way. 'I saw the most gorgeous sun dress that would be perfect for you for drinks at the river this afternoon.'

'What label was it?' Hannah threw her a glance, and Odessa knew she had her hooked. Now to reel her in.

'It was a Minko. A patchwork maxi. It was just you, darling.'

'Ooh, you're bad. I suppose we'd have time for a quick champers at the wine bar across the road from Harrods too. Just one, of course.'

'Of course. But honestly, I'd be fine to drive too. Who's going to pull us up in the hedgerows of Berkshire? We can open the top once we get off the motorway.'

'How much was the dress?' Hannah asked as she took one hand off the steering wheel to smooth her already perfect hair. 'I had two flat tyres yesterday and Daddy took them out of my allowance. And no to driving, and no to the top down. I paid out a fortune at the hair salon this morning.'

'You can afford it. If you're short, I can loan you. Now turn left at the next street. Daddy's office is on the left, halfway down.'

'Are you telling me you haven't packed a formal dress in one of those three suitcases in the boot?' Hannah grinned and did as she was bid. 'Okay, I guess another couple of dresses won't hurt. Gran does like everyone to dress formally for dinner. Tonight too.'

'I've already worn both the dresses I've packed. I need a buzz and a new dress or two will give me that.'

'I thought coming to the estate for the weekend would cheer you up. I had noticed you've been a bit quiet lately.' Hannah flicked the left indicator on, and Odessa smiled. Although they'd been friends since boarding school, Hannah's family were higher up the social ladder than Odessa's.

Nouveau riche, Odessa had been called. She'd overheard Clarissa, one of the women in their group talking about her father's company one night.

Clarissa was a bitch, so Odessa hadn't let it bother her.

'I'm so excited that you managed to get me invited to your gran's party. Such a great group of people will be there.'

'I asked Gran if I could invite our whole set. She was happy to have the young crowd there.'

'That's good. It's hard to believe she's going to be seventy,' Odessa said. 'She's still gorgeous.'

'She is. I hope I have her genes.'

Odessa rolled her eyes. 'There's no doubt of that.'

'I might look like her, but I'm not driven like she is. Gran has no need to work, but she's still running her PR company, you know.' Hannah laughed. 'She keeps telling me I need to get a job. I'm sure I'll get another lecture this weekend about work or study.' She shook her head. 'Now why would I need to do that?'

'I remember the time we both got suspended from Mayhew, and we got sent down to your gran for a serious talking to.' Odessa giggled as she remembered. 'She told us every young woman has particular talents, and the staff at Mayhew see it as their job to help her find and develop them.'

'You've discovered yours, Essie darling. I'm still looking.'

'What work skills have I got?'

Hannah shot a laughing glance her way as she turned into the narrow street. 'You have a talent for drinking champagne, looking gorgeous, and attracting the best-looking men in London. I'm surprised you haven't nabbed one by now.'

'Turn at the building with the black wrought iron gates open on the left.' Odessa ignored her friend's frivolous summing up of her talents. It rankled; maybe it was time she did something with her life. The one thing she had taken away from school was the discovery that she had a talent for jewellery design. Working with fine silver and designing unique pieces had appealed, until she'd tried to find work in the field. Everywhere she'd tried had suggested starting out as a sales assistant. Serving in the store and making coffee for the designers.

Not for her. Maybe one day she'd start her own business. But while she was young, there was too much fun to be had. One day, she'd make use of the knowledge she'd learned in the silversmith course she'd done. She was sure Daddy would help; he'd be pleased to see her doing something. Both her parents would.

Odessa couldn't see the point in working, and she'd never mentioned her creative interest in jewellery to her friends. Her family had enough money to keep her in the style to which she had become accustomed to. Occasionally she made a token effort and worked for a while, but it always interfered with the things she wanted to do. Since her best friend, Rafe, had moved away to some tiny island off Australia, she'd lost focus.

Rafe had given her a talking to before he left. 'It's time you grew up, Odessa. Your father spoils you rotten, but one day you'll get bored with swanning around looking beautiful, and not doing anything useful,' he'd said.

'You think I'm beautiful?' she'd asked with what she hoped was a coquettish look from beneath her lashes.

'You know you are. I don't need to tell you that.'

'Well, why are you going away? Don't you love me?' Odessa had pouted.

'Of course I love you, like a little sister. And I worry about you as much as your parents do.'

'But why are you moving away? I need you.'

Rafe stared past her, and she saw a dark despair in his eyes, a despair that she didn't understand. Odessa had met his ex-wife and knew Rafe was better off without her. He should know that too.

'Because I must.'

'And you won't get bored away from here? Living on a tiny speck in the ocean? Sorry, darling, but I disagree.' Odessa knew it was Rafe's divorce that was making him run away. She knew she had to wait until he got over it, and came back to England, and then he'd realise that she was the best woman for him. She knew she was; he just had to realise that fact. Absence makes the heart grow fonder and all that.

Hannah parked the luxury car very carefully and checked it was locked when they were standing in the small parking area. 'I won't get booked here, will I?'

'No, I'll sort it with Daddy if there's a problem. I don't want to go in now, though. He'll think I've listened to him. He's been trying to put me to work in the family business for a couple of months.'

'Let's go shopping.' Hannah looked down at the Cartier watch on her wrist. 'We have forty-five minutes to shop and have one quick drink. There's a wine bar on the corner across from Harrods.'

Odessa's grin was cheeky. 'We can be a teensy bit late and make an entrance at Swallowfield House, can't we?'

'We can, and I'll be in my new Minko dress. That's an excellent idea, Essie. Maybe we'll have time for two drinks!'

##

An hour and a half later, Hannah tugged at Odessa's arm as she talked to the barman in the Green Vine Wine bar.

'Sweetie, we really have to leave, or we'll miss the pre-dinner drinks by the river at Gran's.'

Odessa smiled across the bar. 'We'll come back in for a drink on the way home on Sunday, Oliver.'

Odessa's smile grew as he reached over and took her hand. 'I'll look forward to it.'

Hannah was waiting by the door as Odessa tucked Oliver's card into her pocket.

She curled her lip. 'A barman? Your standards are slipping, darling.'

'He was an interesting guy. He's doing a law degree, and it's only a part-time job.'

'If he needs to work while he's at university he's not the man for you. And'—Hannah's smile was sly—'he was a teensy bit young too.'

Odessa lifted her chin. 'Don't be a bitch.'

'Well, we are almost thirty, and he looked like he was just out of school.'

Depression settled over Odessa like a wet blanket and her interest in the weekend ahead sank like a stone in the Thames. She should have stayed home. 'Let me drive, Han? We'll never get there at the rate you drive. And you can look at all your shopping.' She watched as Hannah stowed a dozen shopping bags on the back seat.

Hannah shook her head. 'No. Daddy would kill me if I let you.'

'Come on, how will he know?'

Hannah stared at her as she considered the offer, but finally shook her head again. 'No, he'll be at Gran's when we drive in or he might pass us on the way. I'll drive. I can't afford to lose my allowance, and he's been threatening more often lately. Daddy wants me to get a job too.'

'What is it with our parents?' Odessa opened the passenger door.

'They simply don't know what's important when you're young.' Hannah started the car and pulled out onto the A4 and headed towards Hammersmith.

'Shite, Han. Look out. You pulled out in front of a lorry.'

'He stopped,' Hannah replied, but her voice shook a little. 'I hate driving in the peak hour traffic and Friday afternoons are the worst.'

'Well, you know the solution. I can have us in Swallowfield in an hour, and you can relax.'

'Oh, all right, you win. I'll pull up after the Chiswick flyover and you can take over.'

Odessa smiled. It never took much to get Hannah to give in.

The two young women were lost in their own thoughts as they headed towards the M4. Odessa tried to shake off the strange blackness that had descended on her. Once she was driving, she would be able to focus on the road, and chase those dark thoughts away.

Hannah pulled over as promised and they swapped sides. Odessa took over, and the Aston Martin surged along the M4.

'I wish I had your confidence. If I drove that fast, I'd run off the road,' Hannah said.

'I'll teach you how to drive properly on the way home.'

'No, I'm not game,' Hannah said as she reached across to the back seat and pulled some of the shopping bags onto her lap. 'Oh, I adore these earrings. They'll match the dress perfectly. I'm so pleased you spotted them.'

'I love the shoes. The colours are gorgeous. How much did you end up spending?' Odessa changed back a gear and the car roared past two lorries.

'Oh, Essie. I'm not game to add it up. Probably over a thousand pounds. Thank God for credit cards.'

'And fathers,' Odessa said drily. 'Anyway, you'll look gorgeous. Now remind me where to turn off to Swallowfield.'

'You take the left exit off the junction after Whitely Wood. I'll tell you when we get there.'

'Ha, fat chance. You'll have your nose stuck in those shopping bags. I think I remember.' She reached over and flicked on the screen of the Sat Nav.

Half an hour later they turned off the motorway.

'Yes, I remember now. Three Mile Cross is where I head to your Gran's.' Odessa slowed the speed as the road narrowed.

'Don't go too close to the hedgerows. We can't turn up with scratches on the car.'

'Just chill, sweetie. Trust me.'

'Oh and I forgot to mention, don't call Gran, "Gran". Now that she's seventy she's decided she wants to be called Vivian.' Hannah put her head back and closed her eyes as they travelled the last few miles.

'Oh shit,' Odessa exclaimed as they turned into the narrow lane that led to Swallowfield Hall.

'What's wrong. Did you scratch the car?'

'No, worse than that. Look!'

'Oh, fuckety-fuck. I'm dead.' Hannah groaned as she spotted her father walking along the side of the lane with two black Labradors bounding ahead.

Odessa gulped. 'Is it too late to swap seats?'

'Yep, he's already seen us. Oh shit.' Hannah shoved as many of the shopping bags as she could beneath the seat. 'I know, I'll say we swapped over in the lane because I wanted to get changed.'

'Good luck with that.'

They both waved as they passed him, and by the look of his face, Odessa knew Hannah was going to have to sweet-talk her way out of this own.

It didn't bother Odessa. She'd loved driving the Aston Martin down the motorway. Hannah hadn't realised, because she'd been dozing, but Odessa had clocked over a hundred and ten miles per hour when she'd overtaken a couple of cars travelling slowly in the middle lane. Speed gave her a better rush than alcohol did. And you didn't end up with a hangover.

'Pull over at the carriage house before we go up to the main house, and we can freshen up. I want to put my new dress and earrings on.'

'Don't forget the shoes.' Odessa stood beside the car while Hannah went inside. She brushed her fingers through her hair and pulled out her lipstick.

Even though she'd said she was excited to be here, Odessa really wasn't looking forward to the weekend anymore, and she couldn't be bothered getting changed for drinks and then again for dinner.

But maybe it was better than the alternative of being home alone in her flat.

Same old crowd, drinking too much in the early evening spent by the river, sharing all the latest gossip. Champagne. She'd probably end up sleeping with Charlie Cochrane, because it was the easiest way to get him to stop nagging her to marry him.

God, we're a shallow bunch, Odessa thought. Even though Hannah was a friend, she still wouldn't trust her to be there if she ever really needed support.

None of the girls in the group were close. Most of them were worried about being the prettiest, looking the best and snaffling the best-looking guy. Scrap that, the richest guy, she thought with a grin. And that was Charlie.

With a sigh Odessa walked around to the passenger side when Hannah came out of the house.

'Well?' she asked, twirling around to show off the new dress.

'Gorgeous,' Odessa replied. 'You'll have them all salivating over you, even Charlie with a bit of luck.'

'Oh no, Charlie's all yours.'

'I don't want him. Come on let's get this to-do with your father over and then we can go and have a drink.'

Chapter 2

Pippa and Rafe's wedding
Pentecost Island
November

The music that Sienna had playing on low volume in the day spa went a little way to calming me. I lay back and closed my eyes as Evie massaged my scalp over the basin; the scent of coconut shampoo surrounded me. Sienna had a schedule for the afternoon; she ran Hebe, the day spa like an army general.

I was with Evie for my hair first, while Sienna did Tam and Nell's makeup. Then Sienna had insisted that when they were finished, makeup and hair done, they would leave and not see me until I was dressed and they walked me through the rainforest to my wedding.

My thoughts turned to what was ahead today. Not having any family to see me married, or a father to give me away, left a little corner of my heart sad. Losing my parents at a young age had come at an emotional cost that I had only recently learned to cope with. I had adored my dad, and although I was sad that he wasn't here to give me away today, I had no sense that he or my mother were watching down on me, but in my heart I knew Aunty Vi was.

'Are you a little nervous, Pip?' Evie asked as she rinsed off my hair. 'I could feel the tension through your scalp.'

'No, just a little bit sad. Thinking about my parents and my aunt. No family to cheer me along on my wedding day.' I didn't want to say anything about the doubts that had surfaced before. I'd done my best to push them aside.

Evie walked around to the front of the basin. 'Jed and I didn't have any family there either. We were married in a registry office in a country town, and we had one friend each as a witness.' She laughed as she towelled my hair and then wound it around in a turban. 'And we went to the pub for our reception. Look at you and your wedding! Getting married on your own tropical island and being pampered in a day spa.'

I nodded and the towel around my hair wobbled as I sat up. 'I know. I am so lucky. And it's going to be a wonderful day.'

'It is. And remember you're surrounded by friends who love you like a sister.' She nodded to the schedule that Sienna had written up on a small whiteboard. 'I'll dry your hair, and then after Sienna does your makeup, I'll style it. Then we'll help you into your dress.'

A cork popped as I walked into the other treatment room. Bubbles cascaded from the bottle of Moët that Tam held up.

'Don't waste it!' I said with a laugh. 'Moët!'

'Nothing but the best for your wedding day.' Tam handed me a crystal flute and I smiled. 'You look gorgeous, Tam.'

Tam nodded. 'Sienna is a magician.' She poured four more glasses and handed them around to the girls. 'Just a little bit for me. After all it's a very special day.'

Laughter filled the room as we chatted and Sienna finished Nell's makeup. Nell and Sienna picked up their glasses and we sipped our drinks.

'Where's Eliza?' I asked. 'She should be here too.'

Tam and Nell looked at each other with a smile. 'She's busy. Overseeing the organisation while we get pampered.'

'What's going on?'

'A wedding, silly!' Tam widened her eyes trying to look innocent.

Hmm, I knew her well.

'Don't you worry about anything,' she said. 'We have it all under control.'

'I'm sure you do. I trust my team.' Laughing with the girls had eased my tension, and I finally let go of my worries. 'It's not every day a girl gets married.'

Tam and Nell came over to me before they left.

'How long do we have, Sienna?' Nell asked.

Sienna glanced at her watch. 'It's a quarter to two now, so come back in an hour. Evie and I have our clothes here, so once Pippa is ready, we'll get dressed and head over to the restaurant, ready for you two to walk her over.'

My fingers tingled with excitement and I put the glass down as I held my arms open. 'A hug please, before you go.'

I blinked away tears as my two best friends in the whole world hugged me one at a time.

'Love you, Pippa,' Nell said with a sniff.

'Me too, girlfriend. See you soon.' Tam brushed a tear away before it could spill over.

I swallowed as they left the day spa, and Sienna led me over to the mirror.

##

An hour later, my makeup was done, and Evie had finished my hair, but I remained in the chair as Sienna instructed.

'Just to relax you, not to put you to sleep,' she said as her gentle fingers kneaded my shoulders and neck in a light massage.

'Between that and a glass of bubbles, I probably will go to sleep.' I smiled as serenity and anticipation filled me.

'No, you will not. I will not let you.' Sienna's lilting accent kicked in. She gently wiped the oil from my shoulders. 'It's time to put on the dress. Evie, can you please put that silk scarf over Pippa's hair while we get the dress over her head.'

Sienna crossed the room to where my wedding dress hung beneath a cover on a dress rack. She pulled the cover off and I let out a small gasp.

'I'd forgotten just how beautiful that dress is,' I said staring at it.

'And it will look even more beautiful when you have it on. Come on, my sweet, it's time.'

Chapter 3

Odessa

Berkshire - August

By the time Hannah's father had ranted about his precious car and they made their way down to the river where evening drinks were being held, Odessa was over it.

'It's a car, for fu— for God's sake,' she said to a very contrite Hannah as they opened the gate to the lawn edging the River Blackwater that ran past Hannah's family estate. In the distance Odessa could see the five-arched brick bridge that crossed the river to Swallowfield Park, the seventeenth-century country house next door. Voices and laughter drifted up from the river.

'Yes, but it's Daddy's car. At one point he said he would drive us back to London on Sunday, but then he remembered he had an estate meeting here on Monday, thank God.'

'So we're fine to go back in the Aston Martin?' Odessa asked.

'Yes, but I have to drive.' Hannah shook her head. 'For goodness sake, warn the others not to let on to him that you lost your licence.'

Odessa yawned. 'You know, I think I'll see if I can get a lift back to London tomorrow. I don't fancy spending the whole weekend with the crowd.'

'Don't be silly, Essie. You'll have fun. You always do, and you'll be the life of the party by tomorrow night.'

The friends who'd already arrived were sitting on the lawn outside the small pavilion at the back of the estate. Odessa's mood began to mellow as she inhaled the fresh country air and took the glass of champagne that Charlie held out and sat in the chair that he vacated for her. It was a perfect late summer afternoon, and the air was warm as the sun lowered to the horizon in a dramatic splash of gold and violet. As Odessa sat back and looked up, a flock of geese flew over low enough that the flap of their wings moved the still air and the flurry reached her bare shoulders. To the east, parkland dotted with ancient oaks and silver-trunked beeches climbed to the crest of the hills surrounding the estate. It was so different from the city.

Odessa took a long sip of her champagne and let out a sigh as relaxation began to seep in. Charlie sat at her feet and leaned his head back on her knees.

'Happy, Ess?' he asked with a sweet smile.

She reached forward and ran her hand over his hair. He wasn't as bad as she'd made out. 'I am, Charlie.'

'I could tell you were in a mood, so I was giving you some space.'

'You know me very well.'

'I do.'

If Odessa said the word, Charlie would marry her tomorrow; he'd proposed a few times and been hurt when she'd laughed at him. He'd also been the one to console her when Rafe had left for his tropical island. But she didn't love Charlie that way, and she never would. In the meantime, being friends with benefits suited her fine.

##

The weekend turned out to be enjoyable, but the dark feeling stayed with Odessa. Maybe it was because Rafe wasn't around anymore, or maybe it was because of the glum face that Charlie wore most of Saturday because she'd opted not to share her bed with him the night before.

On Saturday evening before the birthday celebration, they all congregated down by the river. Odessa put her head back and settled into the chair enjoying the warmth of the midsummer sunshine. It wouldn't be long before the leaves were flushed with the gold of autumn.

And another year had passed. It was time to think about her future. Maybe she should just give in and marry Charlie, but she wanted more than that. Her parents had a happy marriage and she knew how much in love they still were. Odessa wanted a marriage like that, and Charlie—as sweet as he was—was only a friend.

A boat puttered past the end of the garden where Hannah's young cousins were playing on the riverbank, their laughter adding to the happy mood as everyone anticipated the party.

Her mother had come back from visiting Rafe a few months ago, raving about the warmth of his island even in the southern winter. Maybe she'd go and visit him soon. She really hadn't thought Rafe would stay there as long as he had; once he'd got over his writer's block and delivered his next book, she'd expected to hear he was coming home.

He hadn't called her for ages, and she was unhappy about that too. Her phone buzzed in the pocket of her summer dress, and Odessa pulled it out and glanced at the caller ID.

'Hello, Mummy,' she said.

'Hi, sweetie, I thought I'd call before the party started.'

Odessa grinned. The party hadn't stopped; it had actually been one nonstop drinking session since they'd arrived last night. That was probably why she was feeling down; too much alcohol had depressed her system.

'What's happening? Is everything okay?' This constant sense of doom sent her into a panic. 'Is Dad okay?'

'Yes, everything's fine. We've had some lovely news and I wanted to share it with you.'

'Someone's hit the Sunday Times bestseller list?'

'No. It's better than that.'

'Wow, you have me guessing. I didn't think there was anything in the publishing world better than that.'

'One of our authors is getting married. And we are very happy about it. And we've been invited to the wedding.'

A cold prickly feeling ran up the back of Odessa's neck. 'Who?'

'Who do you think? There's only one person in our stable of authors who's close enough to be almost family.'

How strange that she'd just been thinking about him. 'Rafe,' Odessa said dully.

'Yes. Isn't it wonderful? After all he's been through, and now he's getting married to an Australian girl. Apparently she owns the other half of the island he lives on.'

'Very convenient. Maybe she just wants him for his land.'

'Odessa! That's not a very nice thing to say. I thought we'd taught you better manners than that. Can't you be happy for him, sweetheart? Daddy and I are delighted for him. He sounds so happy.'

'When's the wedding? Have I been invited too?' She felt like a bitch, but how could she be happy when Rafe was marrying someone else? Just when she'd been thinking about going to see him.

A long silence. 'Ah, it's on the first of November. You're not on our invitation, but I don't expect you would be. Ours arrived yesterday, and I expect yours could be there when you get home.'

'I don't want Rafe to get married. And if I did get invited, I'm not going. I don't want to see him marry some long-legged tanned Aussie bimbo with long blonde hair.'

'Odessa.' Her mother's voice held a warning note. 'You sound about twelve-years-old.'

'Well, I'm not, and I'm not going. I have to go and get ready for the dinner.' She jammed her thumb on the phone with much more pressure than was necessary and disconnected the call.

So that's why she'd been feeling so strange; she must have known. A premonition.

Odessa stood staring at the river as a small sailboat drifted past. When a hand touched her elbow gently, she jumped.

'Are you okay, sweets?' Charlie asked.

'Oh, sod off, Charlie,' she hissed. 'Just leave me in peace.' With that, Odessa turned on her heel and hurried back to her room.

Maybe she wouldn't even go to the formal birthday dinner.

Chapter 4

Rafe
Pentecost Island

Rafe was cleaning up his kitchen after a huge breakfast with Nat and Gabe.

'You'll need energy to get through the day,' Gabe had said as he handed Rafe a plate overloaded with bacon, eggs and sausages with three hash browns on the side. 'How about a beer to wash it down?'

'God, no.' He shook his head. 'I had enough beer last night to do me for a while.'

Gabe and Nat had left to help Eliza, Phillipe and Jed prepare the lawn area for the ceremony this afternoon. As they left, he knew he was grinning like a loon, but the day he'd been waiting for had finally arrived.

Today he was marrying Phillipa, the love of his life. He realised now why his first marriage had never stood a chance. The love that he held for Pippa was the first time he'd ever loved a woman with his heart and soul. He and Rebecca had been too young, and they'd had different ideas about what they wanted out of life, but it had taken Rafe a long time to get over it. Not that she'd left him, but the fact that he'd failed. It had affected his work for a year or more and delayed his publication schedule.

Rafe's phone buzzed on the countertop and his grin widened. He'd known Pippa wouldn't be able to help herself, even though she'd only moved down to the old house yesterday.

Last night had been fun—some light-hearted teasing about losing his freedom, and a few beers, had cemented the friendship with the guys. Phillipe and Jed had come up for the barbeque too but had left before midnight. He'd also invited the new landscape gardener, Dylan, and it had been interesting talking to him about his time in Cornwall.

As Dylan had left last night, he'd offered to help out however he could at the wedding.

'That would be excellent,' Phillipe had said. 'The girls are spreading rose petals along the path through the glade to the lawn, and we want to keep it private for the day and get the guests to use the other path.'

Nat chimed in. 'We didn't want to put up signs, so if you could just hang around the path that leads to the spa hut at the restaurant end from about two o'clock, and redirect anyone who comes that way, that'd be a great help.'

'Consider it done,' Dylan said.

'And if you want to help in the bar, I'm sure they'd appreciate another pair of hands. Just clearing glasses and the like,' Gabe said.

'Not a problem. I've done bar work before.'

Rafe was impressed with Dylan; he was obviously an intelligent guy as well as a hard worker. He'd fitted in well as they'd laughed over a few beers last night. Even though he had only just started work on the island last week, he had the resort looking good, and had mowed the lawns yesterday ready for the wedding. Rafe knew Pippa was pleased with him too. The team on the island was great, and now that Cherry and Angus had sorted out their misunderstanding, everything was going smoothly. For a while there, it had looked as though they might have lost a chef.

Rafe picked up his phone and eyebrows lifted as he read the message.

Surprise!

The message was from his publishers and great friends, Jenny and Bryant; he'd been disappointed when they couldn't come to the wedding.

Jenny and Bryant had been there for him during his divorce. The residual bitterness had drilled a huge hole in Rafe's self-confidence when Rebecca had walked out on him. The move to Australia—to Pentecost Island—had been worthwhile in many ways. His writer's block had gone and he'd produced his next two novels for them. But best of all, he'd met and fallen in love with Phillipa. His smile grew as he scanned the text.

I hope a surprise is okay. We've just landed on Hamilton Island and will be at your wedding.

If there's no room on your island, we will find accommodation here. See you at the wedding. xxx Jenny. P.S. Odessa is with us.

Rafe replied immediately. **Very happy to hear that. Welcome! We will find accommodation.**

He'd call down to Nell as soon as he'd finished cleaning the kitchen. Even if the huts were full—but he was sure they weren't—Bryant, and Jenny and Odessa could stay in the house tonight, Rafe was sure Pippa wouldn't mind. He'd also let Angus know there would be three extras in the restaurant. Rafe was smiling as he went back to the kitchen and finished his chores.

Chapter 5

Dylan - Pentecost Island

Just before two o'clock, Dylan Nash had a quick shower and dressed in clean shorts and pulled a *Ma Carmichael's Resort* polo shirt over his head. He hummed beneath his breath as he hurried from the bathroom that he shared in the building at the back of the original house with Angus, one of the chefs. Being offered the job on Pentecost Island had made him very happy. So far, he'd liked everyone he'd met in his first week, and everyone had been very welcoming. The island had a great vibe to it.

Being invited up for a barbeque at Rafe's last night had been unexpected, but he'd soon found acceptance as one of the guys and not just a staff member. Nat and Gabe explained their relationship to the partners on the island, as did Phillipe, the Frenchman, who pointed out his yacht riding at anchor out in the bay.

The handover of the landscaping role from Evie had gone smoothly, and Dylan already had some new ideas for the resort gardens. He'd walked around the island on his second day and had been impressed. What Evie had achieved in a few months was admirable.

'I'll be over on the mainland, just north of Mackay,' Evie had said as she showed him where the equipment was kept in a building adjacent to his accommodation. 'Jed and I have bought a property near Calen, so it's not far to come over here for a day occasionally if you ever need a hand.'

'I'll be taking you up on that,' he said. 'I've seen the order for the outdoor furniture that Jed is making for the bar, so I'm sure you'll need to come over here.'

'Don't hesitate to call if you need to know anything either. Jed and I will be here until the day after the wedding, and then we're back to Brisbane to get packed up for the move.' She handed him a card with her mobile and email. 'I love Pentecost Island, and I'll be back as often as I can.'

As Dylan walked the back path, he stopped a few times and moved a couple of small branches from the glade where seats wrapped around the trunk of one of the large hoop pines. This was a lesser used path to the bay, but the guests would be using it for the rest of the day. Once he reached the day spa, he took the right fork and headed to the reception area, smiling at what the girls had done.

The path was strewn with red rose petals and luckily so far, the breeze hadn't come up and blown them off the path, but he was sure that would happen later in the afternoon. By then the wedding would be in full swing and he'd be helping in the bar. Tealight candles flickered beneath glass covers on both sides of the path; he knew Tam and Nell had done it as a surprise for Pippa. He walked along checking that all the candles were still alight. As he reached the end of the path where it led to the restaurant, a couple in swimming costumes were about to head that way down to the beach.

'Hi there,' he said. 'If you don't mind, I'll ask you to take the other path. This one is closed for the wedding party to use for an hour or so.'

'Certainly.' The man nodded and Dylan directed them to the other path.

Dylan went back to pick up a couple of large twigs that he'd noticed as he'd heard the couple coming. As he approached the curve in the path, he bent to pick up a branch and was about to straighten when someone barrelled into him, almost knocking him off his feet.

Before he could speak, he was subjected to a mouthful of vitriol delivered in a shrill voice, at odds with the plummy English accent.

'What the hell do you think you're doing? I almost fell and that's the last thing I need.'

'I'm sorry, madam, but this path is closed for the wedding.' He kept his tone pleasant, despite her attitude. 'I'm sorry you didn't see me.'

'Are you blaming me?' She looked at the logo on his shirt. 'I'm assuming you're staff?'

He stared at the woman as she attempted to push past him. 'This path is closed, madam.'

'How dare you. I'll go where I please. Move.'

Dylan gently took her arms and turned her to face back the way she had come, still keeping his voice civil. 'The path is closed as there is a wedding this afternoon. The other one there will take you to the beach.'

'How dare you touch me. I'll report you to Rafe. And of course I know there's a bloody wedding.'

'I've been instructed to keep this path clear for the bridal party.' Dylan let go of her and stood in the centre of the path with his arms folded. Even though she was tall, he towered over her.

She lifted her chin and stared at him. 'I am a guest at this bloody wedding, and I need to speak to the bride, so step aside. Now.'

'No.' Dylan wondered if he was doing the right thing, but he didn't like her attitude or her 'bloody wedding' comment. Something was wrong here.

'Odessa!' Dylan looked past the woman when he heard Rafe's voice. As he looked back at her, her expression had changed, and tears now welled in her eyes. 'Oh, Rafe. Thank goodness you're here. This man just assaulted me.' Her voice held a contrived shake that hadn't been evident a moment ago.

Rafe took the woman's arm. 'Come back to the house, please. You're not to bother Pippa.'

Dylan couldn't believe it when she stamped her foot. He'd never witnessed such a performance from a grown woman. He'd had his own problems with Siobhan, but his ex had been able to manipulate without resorting to tantrums, and he'd fallen for it every time. He'd learned a lot about women in the six months before his wife had left, and judging by her behaviour this one had an impressive range of tactics in her repertoire

He watched, fascinated as the woman looked up at Rafe and her whole demeanour changed. Along with her voice, her expression softened. She was a very attractive woman, pale skin and dark hair, her large blue eyes were framed with thick lashes.

'I just wanted to meet her and tell her how happy I am for her, darling.'

'I'm sure you do.' Rafe's voice was dry as he glanced at Dylan and took the woman's arm. 'Thanks, Dylan. I appreciate your work.'

'Are you taking his side? That . . . that gorilla? He manhandled me.'

'I'm sure he didn't. He was doing his job. Now you have one more chance. Come to the house and be reasonable or I will have no hesitation in putting you on a boat and sending you straight back to Hamilton Island.'

'No,' she said in a childlike voice.

'For fuck's sake, this is the very reason why you didn't get an invitation to the wedding.

Dylan widened his eyes when Rafe lost his cool.

'And don't go hiding behind what happened.' Rafe's voice was cold. 'You've always been a spoilt brat, Odessa. Look, I'm sorry for what you've been through. It's awful, and I'm more than happy for you to stay here and recover, but on one condition. I am not going to let you hurt Pippa. I am not going to let you ruin our wedding day. Is that clear?'

'You're a bully, and I hate you.' Again, the foot stamp, but this time the woman called Odessa started to cry.

Dylan was surprised when Rafe put his arms around her. As he gently patted her back, Rafe caught Dylan's eye.

'Thanks, mate. I'll get you to keep an eye on the path. If you see anything untoward'—he inclined his head towards the woman in his arms—'do what you have to do. I'll deal with the consequences. Now I have to go and get ready. Can't be late for my wedding. Not a good look. Especially now.'

Dylan nodded, watching as Rafe led her away.

All he could hope was that she didn't come back.

Chapter 6

Odessa
Berkshire - August

Odessa's mood had improved after a couple of glasses of champagne. She caught sight of herself in the large mirror on the southern wall of the ballroom. The red figure-hugging dress that she'd bought at Harrods on their stop yesterday afternoon had been worth every penny, even if it meant she'd have to hit Dad up for another loan to get her through the month. The sequins along the edge of each shoulder sparkled as she moved closer to the group of her friends who were sitting on a curved seat in the corner. Clarissa sent her a sweet smile and she gave an equally false one in return.

Charlie jumped up to make a space for her and she reached up and kissed his cheek. 'Sorry I was such a cow this afternoon, sweets.' Her temper had only lasted a few minutes and then she'd felt bad for being mean to Charlie. As long as Rafe was truly happy, that was all that mattered. She'd just have to get used to it, and hope he wasn't making another mistake. Men, they never knew what was good for them.

Charlie's fingers brushed her cheek. 'You're forgiven. You do look ravishing, Odessa.'

'Ravishing? Now that's a word with connotations.'

He grinned and put his arm around her, and she leaned against Charlie, and whispered, 'Rafe's getting married.'

'Is that good news?' he asked carefully.

'I guess it is for him,' she said. 'But as long as he's happy, I suppose I can be happy for him.'

'I'm pleased, if you are,' he said carefully.

'I'm happy.' She nudged him. 'Now are you going to get me another drink?'

Even though the night was lively, and the music was geared more to their generation than Hannah's grandmother, Odessa felt apart and on edge. She was thoughtful, and realised it was because she was tired of this partying; drinking never-ending champagne, constant gossip and laughing at things that really held no amusement for her. Hearing Rafe's news had been a wake-up call; her reaction had been immature. She knew full well that there was no romance between them, but she had let herself dream.

But when she finally chose a man, he would be like Rafe. A gentleman, and steady and true. But first, she was going to get her career sorted. It was past time that she settled down.

##

Breakfast the next morning was more of the same. A huge table was set in the conservatory, and the buffet was loaded with English breakfast food. Odessa turned her nose up at the black pudding and mushrooms that Charlie was loading onto his plate as she reached for a piece of toast.

Taking a seat opposite Hannah, Odessa shook her head when a white-jacketed waiter offered to add champagne to her orange juice. 'No, thank you, just juice for me.'

'What time do you want to go back to the city?' she asked Hannah.

'This morning,' Hannah said sipping her champagne. 'I'll only have the one drink and it's watered down anyway, so it won't take long to wear off.'

'Can I cadge a lift too?' Charlie sat beside Odessa, his plate holding scrambled eggs and bacon, two grilled sausages, hash browns, black pudding, mushrooms and tomatoes all covered with a layer of baked beans.

'Charlie, that is just gross,' she said nibbling on her toast. 'Talk about clogging your arteries.'

He laughed as he shovelled a forkful of food up. 'Hey, this is what my grandfather has every day, and he's almost ninety. A breakfast like this every day should see me live to a hundred.'

Odessa finished her orange juice and stood. 'Well, I'm going for a walk along the river and then I'm going to pack. What time, Han?'

'Say ten-thirty?' Hannah lifted her glass for a refill as the waiter hovered.

Odessa raised her eyebrows. 'Looks like I'm driving back to London.'

Hannah glanced at her father three seats along, but he was talking. 'Ssh. And no.'

'I can drive,' Charlie said.

'Would you two please be quiet,' Hannah grumbled in a low voice.

Odessa grinned and headed outside. She was surprised to see Hannah's grandmother sitting on a deck chair on the grass. She crossed over and knelt beside her. 'Everything okay? Have you had a lovely party?'

'Hello, darling.' Vivian's hand reached out to Odessa's arm, her diamond rings sparkling in the sunlight. 'We haven't had a chance to catch up yet. What are you doing?'

'I was going to take a stroll along the river.'

'May I join you or would you prefer solitude?' Vivian's eyes were shrewd.

'Please come.'

They strolled past the pavilion and stood together on the riverbank without speaking. The clear water below babbled over the rocks and small fish darted about the rocks. A couple of dragonflies hovered over the water and their green bodies glinted in the sunlight.

Vivian linked her arm through Odessa's. 'So, tell me what you've been doing lately.'

'Not a lot.'

'I've noticed you seemed extra quiet this weekend.' Vivian's soft hand squeezed Odessa's.

'I know it was your birthday celebration, but this weekend has made me realise that I need to do something. Han and I were talking about our talents on the way down, and we remembered that talking to you gave us when we were at Mayhew.'

'And what have you decided?"

'I'm going to do what I know I'm good at. I'm going to try to start a career in silversmithing. Making jewellery.'

'That's a career that takes skill, as well as time and patience.'

'I know, but I'm sure I can do it, if I apply myself. And it's time I did.'

'I have a friend who has a son in jewellery production. Do you have your phone with you?'

Odessa nodded.

'Text me your number and I'll send the contact to you. And I'll have a word to my friend.'

'Thank you, Vivian.' Odessa took out her phone and texted her contact details to the number that Vivian recited. 'Thank you so much.'

'Dedication, darling. That's what it takes.' She tapped her nose with an elegant finger. 'And the right contacts.'

##

After she and Vivian had returned to the house, Odessa hurried up to her room, and packed her bag. This was a weekend for tying up loose ends. On the way back to London she would tell Charlie they were finished. Or to be fair, tell him to go and find a girl who would value him, and not use him for her own ends.

Hannah and Charlie were waiting at the car when she went downstairs. Hannah's eyes were glittering, and her cheeks were flushed.

'How many champagnes have you had?' Odessa asked suspiciously.

'Only two. Watered down with juice.' Hannah's gaze slid away.

'I think I should drive,' Odessa said with a frown.

'No, Daddy's watching from upstairs. Don't look up.'

'Okay. Maybe we can change over.' Odessa handed the first of her suitcases to Charlie who hoisted it into the boot. 'The other two are in the foyer. I'll go and get them.'

'I'll go.' Charlie said and loped up the drive.

When he came back, Odessa offered to sit in the back. 'There'll be more leg room for you in the front,' she said.

'Thanks, but no,' Charlie said. 'I'm going to have a kip in the back seat. You can talk to Han and keep her awake.'

The motorway was busy, and Odessa was a nervous passenger as Hannah constantly changed from the left lane to the middle lane.

'Just be careful. If you're going to stay in the middle lane, you need to go a bit faster.

Hannah turned her head. 'No, I'd rather be in the left, and go slow. I can't concentrate when there are cars and lorries on both sides of the car.' She swung back the car back into the middle lane.

'Shit, Han, watch the traffic. You nearly ran up the back of that lorry.'

'Sorry, but he's spooking me. He keeps changing lanes and tooting at me because I'm going slow.'

'Pull up at the next service area, and I'll take over. Unless you want to drive, Charlie?' Odessa glanced over to the back seat. Charlie was asleep, his mouth open and he was snoring softly. As Odessa turned back to the front, Hannah let out a piercing scream. The Aston Martin drifted into the left lane and as she wrenched the steering wheel to the right, there was a sudden loud bang, followed by the terrifying sound of grinding metal.

Odessa looked past Hannah as she tried to control the car. Her eyes were wide, and her fingers were white where she gripped the wheel. The car was heading back towards the lorry that had clipped the driver's side. There was another loud bang and Odessa's head whipped back and hit the head rest as the Aston Martin slammed into the lorry. Pain seared through her neck and her vision blurred, and then the world went black.

Chapter 7

Odessa
August - London

The pillow was firm beneath Odessa's head, harder than her pillow at home. She'd have to tell Vivian about the hard pillows. Or was she somewhere else? She knew she'd been at Swallowfields, but her head was heavy, and she couldn't open her eyes. And her neck was hurting.

The traffic past the house was very loud and Odessa couldn't figure out why. The estate was a long way from the motorway. Random thoughts flitted in and out of her head as she tried to wake up. Forcing her eyes open was impossible, and she lifted her hands to her face. Her fingers came away wet and sticky, but she still couldn't see anything.

Maybe she'd drunk too much last night?

I must wake up, she tried to say but no words came out.

Time was of the essence because they were going back to London today, and she was going to start her new life like she'd told Vivian.

She was going to help me, Odessa thought. She gave me something. But she couldn't remember what it was.

She frowned and tried to lift her head, and then remembered she'd already been out of bed once. She'd had breakfast, and then she'd talked to Hannah's grandmother after that.

Gritting her teeth Odessa forced her eyes open and was relieved to see Hannah next to her. Her eyes were wide, and she was staring at Odessa. Cold trickled through her and her vision blurred but she kept looking back at Hannah.

'Why are you looking at me like that, Han? What's wrong?'

Panic built in her chest as the events of the past few minutes came back and she stared at Hannah, but her friend didn't move, and her eyes stayed wide.

A sob rose in Odessa's chest and voices reached her. 'Two deceased. One in and out of consciousness. Second ambulance is two minutes away.'

'Don't move, love. Close your eyes.' Gentle gloved hands held her arms. 'We just have to check you over and then we'll get you out.'

'Out of where?' she whispered 'Let me go back to bed. I don't want to wake up.' Her voice rose shrilly. 'Why is Hannah here? Where's Charlie.' The sob broke in her throat and she drew in deep gasping breaths.

The lorry.

Hannah's lane changing. Charlie's snoring Her yelling at Hannah.

She'd been in an accident. They had said that there were two deceased, and she knew she wasn't one of them.

'No, no.' Odessa put her hands on either side of her head and tried to move it from side to side in denial, but excruciating pain shot up her neck and into her head.

Maybe I'm dying too.

##

When Odessa woke next, Hannah wasn't staring at her. She would never forget that as long as she lived. There was silence now and the bed was soft beneath her back. She could smell that awful hospital smell that she'd hated. Ever since Daddy had taken her to see his father—her granddad—when he was dying, she'd hated that smell, and had never visited anyone in hospital since. Not even for new babies when her friends delivered.

I wasn't interested in babies anyway, she thought vaguely. Or parties, anymore.

'Odessa?' The familiar voice calmed her as her thoughts took a dive.

'Daddy,' she murmured but no sound came out. Odessa lifted her hand and immediately it was engulfed in her father's smooth grasp.

She knew it was Daddy. His hands were soft from working in the office all day.

'It's okay, sweetheart.'

'Am I going to die too?'

His voice caught and she heard him swallow. 'No, you're going to be fine. You have a neck injury. We can probably take you home tomorrow.'

'Yes, please.' She drifted back to sleep but when she woke up a while later, her father was still holding my hand. 'Is it true, Daddy? Or are Han and Charlie in hospital too? Did I dream that . . . that . . . that they died in the car?' She managed to open her eyes and was distressed to see his mouth working, and his eyes were wet with tears.

'We'll talk about it when you're better.'

Odessa knew then that she hadn't dreamed any of it.

Hannah and Charlie were dead, and it was her fault.

I should never have let Hannah drive, she thought, as huge wracking sobs rose in her chest.

Chapter 8

Pippa
Pentecost Island - the wedding

Sienna and Evie slipped my wedding dress over my head, and I laughed as the silk scarf tickled my neck when Evie whipped it off with a "ta da".

'Oh my God, look at you,' Evie said with her hand on her chest. 'Absolutely stunning.'

Sienna let out a soft sigh as she stared at me. 'You are exquisite, ma cherie.'

I stood there feeling almost surreal as Tam and Nell came through the door, each carrying a small posy of yellow-centred frangipani. Nell lifted one hand up to her mouth, and as Tam stared at me, tears welled in her eyes.

'So beautiful,' she mouthed, shaking her head. 'Oh Pippa, it's just perfect.'

When I'd found the dress on Hamilton Island, I knew it was the one before I even tried it on. It was one of those moments when I just knew it was meant to be. The plain white silk clung to me like a second skin. I'd lost a little bit of weight since we'd been on the island and my olive skin now had a permanent glowing tan. The only embellishment on the dress was Spanish lace around the fitted bodice and the low cut back that plunged to just below my waist. The bare skin of my back was crisscrossed by fine narrow straps.

My smile was shaky as I acknowledged Tam and Nell resplendent in matching ivory silk dresses. With her other hand Tam held out a single white cattleya orchid to me. The strong spicy aroma filled the room.

In the absence of any family—no, I wasn't going to feel sorry for myself—Tam and Nell were doubling up as my attendants as well as giving me away.

'Look at you pair. You both look gorgeous.' My voice didn't sound like me.

'Evie and I will be very fast to get changed and then we all are ready,' Sienna said, her words formal as she quickly poured us a glass of champagne. 'You must not be late.'

I smiled but my hand was shaking as I lifted the glass to my lips. The warmth of the emotion in the room settled over me like a soft cloak.

'Don't wreck your lipstick,' Tam said, her voice husky.

Nell brushed the back of her hand over her eyes. 'I thought you'd like to know that the English guests are in two huts. Luckily we had three empty, due to a late cancellation. Dylan helped move their luggage down from the house about half an hour ago.'

'So you and Rafe will have the house to yourselves tonight,' Tam added.

I couldn't help the giggle that escaped. I'm sure it was relief. 'No different to every night for the past few months, since I moved in with him.'

'Yes, but this is your wedding night. Anyway it's all sorted,' Nell added.

'Thanks for that.'

After Sienna and Evie got changed, and headed off, it wasn't long before we were ready to walk through the forest to the restaurant. The ceremony was being held on the lawn outside the new building.

'Where's Eliza?'

'She's making sure everything is right.' Tam grinned. 'She didn't trust any of the guys to do it properly.'

'So, are you ready to go get married?' Nell drew a deep breath and put her glass on the small table near the door. She and Tam picked up their posies, and Tam passed me the orchid that had been placed on the table.

'I am.' I caught sight of myself in the mirrored wall behind the counter where Sienna took the bookings. I wasn't wearing a head piece. My pale auburn hair had grown over the past year and Evie had curled it into long ringlets and then caught them up high on the back of my head so that the curls fell down past my shoulders.

Sienna had worked her magic with my makeup. My green eyes looked larger and were tipped at the corners with the skilful use of a pale eyeliner. My cheeks were slightly flushed, and I knew that wasn't makeup, but from the anticipation curling in my stomach.

'Let's go to a wedding,' I said.

Tam led the way, and Nell was behind me as we stepped out onto the veranda at the front of the hut. If it was possible the morning's weather had improved from perfect to magical. There wasn't a breath of wind and the water in our bay shone like a roll of blue silk. To the west, cumulonimbus clouds rose high in the sky, and white fragments of clouds drifted lazily in the sky high above us.

Eliza waited at the bottom of the two steps holding a basket full of rose petals. 'Beautiful, Pippa.' She blinked away tears.

'Thank you.'

Eliza led the way, and Tam and Nell put their arms through mine.

I let out a tiny gasp as we stepped onto the path. The narrow walkway that led to the glade was covered in red rose petals, and candles on each side of the path flickered in the dim light. The faint sound of classical music drifted through the forest—Rafe had asked that the music be his choice—and I wasn't surprised by the gentle violin music that hovered in the glade. He'd introduced me to his favourite music over the year, and I was learning to love it.

'I hope Rafe's there,' I said nervously.

'He is, and looking just as stunning as you, m'dear.' Eliza put on her Cockney accent.

I shook my head as we walked from the glade to the lawn outside the new restaurant. We were only having a small wedding, so there was no need for the nerves that began to tingle in my limbs as we got closer and the music filled the air around us.

Tam and Nell let go of my hands as we stood on the edge of the lawn, and Sienna and Evie fussed with my dress. Eliza gestured to Philippe in the bar and the music changed to the bridal march.

Goose bumps rose on my arms and my throat closed with emotion as the music swelled.

Rafe turned to look at me, his brilliant blue eyes holding mine as I stood there. I remembered the first time I had seen him in the restaurant at Hamilton Island. It was only a year ago, but it felt like a lifetime. Now I couldn't imagine a life without Rafe in it.

My God. What a beautiful face, I'd thought that night.

Nothing had changed in those months, but I now knew every inch of his skin and loved tracing those features with my fingers each morning as I woke beside him.

Rafe was so good-looking he could have been a movie star. Jet-black hair hung over eyes set wide above chiselled cheekbones. A five o'clock shadow on his olive skin gave him a rakish look. I smiled as I saw the long sleeved pirate-like shirt he wore tucked into dark trousers. The lacing at the front matched the back of my dress. His full lips tilted in a smile as I walked slowly across the emerald green lawn.

There were only two rows of white chairs on each side of the lawn as the gathering was small. Our friends from the island, and their partners, plus Jiminy—who I'd gone to high school with—and his wife, Sarah, and some friends who'd come over from Hamilton

Island. The Riccardo brothers were there, each with a partner; Rafe and I had got to know them well while they worked on our new buildings.

Everyone stood as I followed Tam and Nell down the aisle between the rows of chairs to where Rafe was waiting for me. Several of the guests who were currently at the resort, and the kitchen staff, including Angus and Cherry, stood to one side near the path. Dylan, the new landscaper, was beside them.

I glanced up to the azure-blue sky and sent a silent message. Thank you for bringing me here, Aunty Vi.

I glanced left and right and returned the smiles of our friends as Tam and Nell led me to where Rafe and the celebrant were standing at the front. Three unfamiliar faces looked at me as I looked to the left, two with kind smiles and one pale-faced without a smile.

Rafe's friends. The young woman— Odessa, I assumed—was flanked by her parents and each of them held her arm. A fleeting glimmer of sympathy replaced my happiness briefly as I noticed her pallor and gauntness. She wore a clinging dress and it was easy to see how thin she was.

But I forgot about them as I looked up and saw Rafe's tender smile.

The celebrant gestured to his side and I stepped beside him.

'I love you,' he whispered to me before the celebrant began the ceremony.

Rafe took my hand and held it gently. An exquisite feeling ran through me as I prepared to promise my life and love to this man.

'Good afternoon, everyone, on this glorious Whitsunday afternoon. My name is Catherine Shaw and I am authorised to solemnise marriages according to law. Before Phillipa and Rafe are joined in marriage in my presence and in the presence of these witnesses, I am bound to remind you of the solemn and binding nature of the relationship into which you are now about to enter. Marriage, according to the law in Australia, is the union of two people to the exclusion of all others, voluntarily entered into for life.'

Tam held her hand out for my single orchid before the celebrant spoke the words Rafe had penned and I had chuckled over. Having a world famous author for a husband was sure to mean he would always have the final word. I blinked away tears when Tam and Nell both kissed my cheek before they left me standing with Rafe.

Catherine smiled at both of us. 'I like to get to know the couples I marry, but I can honestly say this is the first wedding I have officiated at where the couple fell in love in a tree during a rescue from a feral goat.'

A wave of chuckles rippled through the gathering, and I couldn't help wondering if Odessa was smiling too.

'As I've spoken to Rafe and Pippa over the past weeks, I have no doubt that this couple have a deep and abiding love for each other. Now before we get to the formal vows, I would like to ask for an affirmation of support from everyone present.'

I froze as Rafe tensed beside me, and I wondered if something was going to happen. Not being able to turn was frustrating, but I refused to let myself be brought down. I squeezed his fingers and looked up at him and held his gaze steadily as murmurs of assent came from behind us.

As Catherine smiled, one lone cloud crossed the sun, and we were cast in shadow. 'Shall we begin?'

We both nodded, and as she spoke, I forgot about the people behind us. I forgot about my past, and I forgot about Rafe's previous marriage. I let my love for Rafe fill me as I prepared to pledge myself to him for the rest of my life.

My eyes stayed on his as Rafe spoke the vows that we had written together.

'Pippa Carmichael, today, I take you as my life partner. From this day, I give to you my heart and my life. My everlasting love and devotion are yours. I promise to cherish you and pledge myself truthfully to you and with all my heart. Forever. Let us share our dreams, thoughts, and lives. Knowing that from this moment, I will have you as my wife fills me with joy. I love you and I will love you forever.'

I blinked away happy tears as joy surged through me and I repeated the words as I made my vow to him. 'Rafe Rendell, today, I take you as my life partner.' I repeated the words that Rafe had written. My voice shook when I came to the final sentence. 'I love you and I will love you forever.'

We exchanged rings and then Rafe's hand gripped mine tightly as Catherine declared us to be husband and wife.

'Now I invite you to share your first kiss as a married couple.'

I lifted my face to his as Rafe's arms went around me and his warm fingers rested on my bare back. The whistles and cheers behind us faded as his lips took mine and he whispered against them.

'Hello, my beautiful wife.'

I lifted my arms and put them around his neck. 'Hello, my gorgeous husband.'

As we kissed the cloud cleared the sun and we were bathed in a shaft of golden sunlight.

Chapter 9

Odessa
Pentecost Island – the wedding

Odessa sat on the hard plastic chair and wished that she'd taken a couple of painkillers as her mother had suggested.

'Just in case, sweetheart,' Jenny had said before they headed from the huts to the lawn. Odessa had been quietly impressed with the accommodation. When the term "hut" had been bandied about when Rafe had explained there was alternative accommodation for them, her expectation had been of something like she'd stayed in on one of those awful school camps in the Lakes District when she was at boarding school. But when they'd been shown to their huts by a woman called Nell, Odessa had been impressed by the unexpected size and quality furnishings, not to mention the incredible view of the bluest water she had ever seen.

If she had to recover somewhere, maybe this was the place to do it. Far away from the memories, and the familiar places, an island where she wouldn't see anyone from her past. Or anyone who had known Hannah and Charlie.

As she thought of them, the ever-present nausea rose, and she put her hand to her mouth.

Her mother leaned over and whispered. 'Are you alright, darling?'

Odessa nodded as her mother pressed a handkerchief into her hand. Despite the threatening tears, she was as "alright" as she could expect to be.

Ever.

She was breathing, and she was alive, and could still function despite the depression that gripped her when she thought of what had passed.

The last minute rush to get to this island in time for Rafe's wedding had been a result of Dr Ennis giving her the all clear to fly. The flight had been exhausting, despite the overnight stop in Singapore.

Maybe coming to Australia to Rafe's island had been stupid, but Odessa knew that her parents had been disappointed when they had told Rafe they couldn't come to his wedding because of the accident. When she'd got the all clear from her doctor, their reaction had convinced her to agree to the trip. She thought if she saw Rafe that everything would switch back to being alright. Even if he was getting married.

Odessa's neck ached and she wriggled in the seat as her darling Rafe stood on the lawn promising to love another woman. She could see why he'd fallen for her—Philippa—she was very beautiful, and her dress would have done justice to one of the exclusive London boutiques that Odessa frequented with Hannah.

Had frequented. Tears welled in her eyes as she corrected herself. Even though it had been eight weeks since the accident, the pain and guilt remained, and she doubted that they would ever leave her.

Her neck pain had eased—it had before that horrendous long flight—but the sadness and the black days would not go away. Her thoughts were chaotic filled with "what ifs". She should have insisted on driving, and then Hannah and Charlie would still be alive. Each time she thought that if she'd been in the back seat instead of Charlie, she would be dead instead of him, her mind would go blank and faintness would overtake her.

The funerals had been horrendous, but Odessa had insisted on attending both. It was the right thing to do. She would never forget the grief on Vivian's face as she had hugged Odessa tightly.

Her parents had organised for her to have a couple of months on the island, and she'd agreed reluctantly. If it had just been Rafe, Odessa would have jumped at the chance, but now he had—or would have in the next five minutes—a wife.

Her temper simmered as the celebrant told Rafe he could now kiss his new wife. Odessa had wanted to check Philippa out before the wedding, and she'd slipped away while her parents were getting dressed. She'd gone looking but had been stopped by that rude guy on the path.

Who needed a bodyguard before a wedding? There was something strange there. It was as though this Phillipa was doing everything she could to make sure that Rafe didn't get away.

Odessa suspected that Rafe had made another poor choice.

If he had, she would be doing something about that.

Odessa looked down as Rafe took his new wife in his arms and kissed her.

Chapter 10

Dylan
Pentecost Island - November

Dylan stood at the edge of the lawn next to the kitchen staff. As soon as the ceremony was over, he would head across to the bar and help out where he could. The wedding ceremony had been pretty good; Rafe and Pippa were obviously in love, and the excitement of their friends around them had been very obvious and contributed to the happy mood.

The atmosphere on Pentecost island was very different to anywhere Dylan had worked before. There seemed to be close relationships and friendships between everyone, and there was a cooperative mood to the place with no obvious hierarchy.

Pippa was the owner and the boss of the resort, but she seemed to work as hard as everyone else did—even last week with the wedding coming up.

Maybe things in his life would change now.

As Pippa and Rafe exchanged their vows, Dylan's gaze shifted to the English woman he'd encountered on the path today. She was obviously a friend, rather than a resort guest since she was at the wedding.

But that didn't matter. He didn't care who she was, he had taken an instant dislike to her, and that surprised him. Dylan was usually easy-going and went with the flow wherever he was, getting on with most people, but that woman and her attitude had fired him up. He'd remained calm with her, but it had made no difference, and he wasn't sure what would have happened if Rafe hadn't come along when he did. She'd got under his skin and he'd felt his temper building when she'd refused to co-operate.

Now his gaze lingered on her where she sat as Rafe and Pippa sat at a small table covered with a white cloth and signed the wedding certificate.

An emerald green dress left the woman's slim shoulders bare and her fair skin translucent. Her dark hair was pulled back in some sort of roll on the back of her head, and her swan-like neck added to the elegance of her appearance. Her eyes were hooded as she stared ahead, and as he watched, she dropped her head and put one hand to her face. The older woman beside her leaned across, obviously comforting her.

So not only rude and ill-mannered, she was not happy about the wedding. It took all kinds, he guessed. He'd had a hard enough time in his life, and it had taught him to not get involved with the crap that some people carried on with. They thought they had it hard, but these days it seemed easier to give in and plead that you couldn't cope, instead of putting your head down and getting on with life.

Dylan well knew what life could throw at you, and you had to move on. There was no point dwelling on the past; it just brought you down.

If he could survive a wedding without falling to pieces, anyone could. He pushed the forbidden memories away and stood straight. He'd left that life behind him, and he planned on making a success of the opportunities on offer here on Pentecost Island. He turned back to look at the woman and scowled as she looked around to see if anyone was paying her attention and then dabbed at her eyes with a lace handkerchief.

An attention seeker too.

No matter how beautiful she was, she held no appeal for him whatsoever; she'd done her dash in the glade this afternoon.

Dylan shrugged and headed for the bar. He had better things to do than wonder what her problem was. And he was annoyed with himself that he'd paid her attention. Hopefully she wasn't staying on the island for long, and he wouldn't run into her again.

Odessa

Odessa took the handkerchief that her mother handed her and looked around to make sure no one had seen her cry. She hated showing emotion like she had been constantly for the past two months; everyone she encountered knew what had happened and wanted to show their sympathy, and when she couldn't stop crying, embarrassment consumed her.

That was one of the best things about being on an island. Rafe—and her parents—were the only ones who knew. Or she hoped that was the case.

A tall woman with curly blonde hair—one of the two who had escorted the bride to the lawn—stepped to the front and spoke above the murmur of conversation. 'Hey everyone, if you'd like to stand, in a couple of minutes we'll clap Mr and Mrs Rendell out as they head down to the beach with the photographer, and then if you'll make your way across to the bar, we'll be serving drinks and canapés on the lawn for the next couple of hours. Dinner will be served at six p.m. in the restaurant over there'—she gestured to a newish looking building on the other side of the lawn—'and then the party starts.' She turned as Rafe and his new wife stood and embraced.

'Woo hoo, everyone, let's show our best to Rafe and Pippa,' the blonde called out. The Australian accent grated on Odessa, but she stood along with the rest of the guests.

She stood back as the bridal couple crossed the lawn, and most of the guests—not that there were many—walked across and hugged them as they offered their congratulations. Her parents stood and joined the throng and she sat back down on the chair. She had all night to meet this Phillipa. Odessa wasn't too keen on spending the next two hours socialising. It was too late to check Phillipa out and get Rafe to change his mind now that they were married. But if she was honest, he did seem to be in love, and he did look really happy.

'Oh, she's lovely,' her mother exclaimed when her parents returned to where Odessa remained sitting.

'That's good. I'll meet her later.'

'Are you okay, love?' Her father leaned down and put his finger under her chin. 'That trip's taken a lot out of you, hasn't it?'

She nodded. 'I think I might go and have a bit of a rest before dinner. I won't be missed. This is *their* day.'

'It is. And it's so good to see Rafe looking so well and happy. He's a different man to the one who left the UK a couple of years ago.'

Odessa covered a pretend yawn, so she didn't have to comment. 'I'm going to go back to the hut. I'll set my alarm so I'm not late for dinner. Okay?'

'Do you want me to come and sit with you?' her mother asked.

Odessa shook her head. 'I'm fine, Mummy. Honestly. Don't worry. I'm just tired from that long trip, and if I have a rest, I'll make it through dinner.'

'All right then. Bryant, you walk Odessa back to her hut.'

'There's no need, Daddy. It's not far.'

'Don't take a sleeping pill, will you? You won't make dinner if you do.'

'I don't particularly want to come to the dinner,' Odessa thought, but she kept her tone sweet. 'I'll have a cup of tea and a nap, and then I'll come back over.' She stood and put her hand up to her aching neck. 'You two go and have some fun.' She gave them a gentle push in the direction of the bar. 'I'm fine. You deserve a break after how you've looked after me for the past two months.'

'Of course we did, sweetheart. And we want to see you recover,' her father said. 'Isn't this the most beautiful setting for healing?'

With a smile, her parents left her. As much as they meant well—and to be honest, they had supported her without a break since the accident—she felt stifled. It would be good when they went home and left her on the island.

She needed space, and she knew she needed time alone to process what had happened.

The noise of the conversations around her were getting louder, and before anyone could talk to her, Odessa put her head down and turned towards the path that led back to the hut she was staying in.

Chapter 11

Pippa
Pentecost Island - the wedding

As the sun set, the light breeze picked up and the fragrance of rose petals filled the air. I still couldn't believe what the girls had done for me, and I wondered how on earth they'd managed to get so many roses over to the island.

My body was light, and the love that surrounded me made me feel like I was walking on air. Rafe's love fulfilled me, but the love of my friends and their determination to give us a memorable wedding day meant so much to me too. It might sound strange, but the happiness that filled me was so strong it almost hurt.

The whole hour we were on the beach having our photos taken Rafe didn't let me go once, and by the look on his face, I knew he was feeling the same as I was.

A bit stupefied, and a little bit disbelieving.

We were married!

As we left the beach to walk back to the restaurant, Rafe's whisper brushed my ear and goose bumps rose on my skin.

'Are you happy, Mrs Rendell?'

'Blissfully so. I don't know if I can take much more.' I put my hand to my chest and reached up to kiss his cheek. 'I'm so happy it hurts.'

'I'll kiss you better.' He turned his head and our lips connected and held.

'Did you know about the roses?' I asked.

He shook his head, but it only increased the movement of his lips on mine. 'I didn't.'

We walked back to the restaurant along the rose-strewn path where the breeze was sending the petals into the air in a flurry. When we reached the lawn, we paused and looked at each other.

'I don't know if I can cope with feeling so happy,' I said.

'Get used to it, babe. This is our life from now on.'

I smiled as my husband's lips brushed mine again.

The guests had broken into small groups and my smile widened as I saw Nat and Nell working together behind the bar. Tam and Gabe were talking to the Riccardos and Gabe's arm was around Tam's shoulder. For the first time I noticed the slight swell of her stomach.

'We probably should mingle, do you think?' I said.

'I'd like you to meet Jenny and Bryant first.' Rafe looked across at the couple who were standing with Eliza and Phillipe. Sienna was standing away to the side by herself.

'I'd like to. I know how much you think of them.'

Rafe took my hand and we joined the four who were chatting. 'Jenny, Bryant, I'd like to introduce Philippa, my wife.' His voice was full of pride.

As Jenny leaned forward and hugged me I was surrounded by the sweet fragrance of a floral perfume. 'It's wonderful to meet you, Pippa. May I call you that? Congratulations, you have got yourself a fine man.'

'I have.'

'And this is Bryant,' Rafe said.

The tall dark man leaned over and kissed my cheek, and Rafe looked around.

'Where's Odessa?'

'She's gone for a rest, but she'll be back for dinner,' Jenny said.

'I'm sorry to hear she's been through a difficult time,' I said.

Jenny reached out and squeezed my hand. 'We appreciate you allowing her to spend some time here. We had to talk her into coming, but I know it will do her the world of good to get away for a while.'

'We'll look after her,' Rafe promised.

'We know you will, but let's not talk about that tonight,' Bryant said.

'Yes,' said Jenny. 'It's your special day and it's a time for celebration. Oh, here comes Odessa now.'

We stood quietly as Odessa crossed the lawn towards us. I was struck by how thin she was. Her emerald green dress was obviously a designer label, but you could see her hip bones through the clinging fabric.

Rafe held one hand out as he held me close with the other. 'Odessa, come and meet Pippa. I hope that you two will become friends.'

When Odessa lifted her head and our eyes connected, I knew immediately that she wanted no friendship with me. Her eyes were cold and empty as they met mine, but when she turned to Rafe, her lips tilted in a smile and her voice was full of warmth. I knew she was here to recover, but I didn't think for one minute that the way she'd looked at me had anything to do with the tragedy.

'That would be lovely. Pippa, I'm so pleased to finally meet you. Rafe kept you a secret from all of us.'

Tam caught my eye, and I could tell she'd seen the look, but I was on my best behaviour.

'I'm pleased that you could get here for the wedding, Odessa. I'm looking forward to getting to know you too. It's so good to meet Rafe's friends. Please make yourself at home on our island.' I kept my voice and smile sweet. I was not going to let a spoilt miss ruin my happy mood or my wedding day. 'Rafe, look. The Riccardos are calling us over.'

As we walked away, I could feel her eyes boring into my back.

I didn't care what was wrong with Odessa Walker. I was holding onto my husband, and I knew I looked good.

I was not going to let one English woman with no manners spoil my wedding.

Chapter 12

Dylan

'Dylan, do you mind if I take Nat off for a quick dance?' Nell, the office manager and one of the bridesmaids, asked as she stood at the bar.

'Of course not. I'm fine here. Go and dance with your lady.' Dylan nodded with a smile. 'I'm happy to take over here. Everyone's right for drinks and it's not busy now that the speeches are done.'

'Did you get something to eat, Dylan?' Nell asked.

'I did. Angus insisted I sat in the kitchen and I had the same meal as you guys did.'

'It was amazing, wasn't it?' Nat opened the half door and walked around to where Nell was waiting.

'Sure was.'

'That dessert that Cherry created was to die for, but I'll need to dance all night to work it off.'

'Thanks, mate, appreciate it.' Nat took Nell's hand and crossed to the small dance floor. Dylan had helped move some of the tables after the meal was cleared away.

Pippa and Rafe had taken to the dance floor for the bridal waltz and after they had done one circuit of the small dance floor, most of the other couples were joining them. After Dylan had helped with bringing the meals out from the kitchen and clearing plates he moved to the bar. A few groups remained chatting at the tables as guests danced, but most glasses were full or half-full.

Dylan was beginning to get a handle on the relationships on Pentecost Island. He frowned as Sienna, the cute woman from the day spa walked over to the bar and climbed up on a stool. She appeared to be the only unattached female on the island, so he would keep himself a bit distant. He had no intention of getting involved in a relationship while he was on the island.

Ever.

This island was so small, it was going to be hard to keep to himself. And there was the fact that it seemed to be perceived as a romantic place. Dylan held a snort back. If you believed in that sort of thing. He had once, but sadly life had shown him the truth.

Sienna sat at the end of the bar looking out over the water. Dylan frowned as he pulled a tray of clean wine glasses from the washer, hoping that she didn't suggest he dance with her.

He'd use the excuse that he wasn't a guest if she did. Her fingers gripped a straw and she stirred the drink that she'd brought over from the table. He kept himself busy cleaning up the bar and rearranging the wine bottles in the fridge.

Eventually he realised how stupid he was being, and his good nature kicked in. He turned and made his way to the end of the bar and was surprised to see the expression on Sienna's face. He'd only spoken to her twice since they'd been introduced when Evie had shown him around the island, but Sienna always had a smile and looked calm and serene. Now as she sat there with her still full glass in front of her, her lips were turned down, and he saw how sad she looked.

'All good for a drink here, Sienna?' he asked quietly as sympathy kicked in.

Her eyes were shimmery as she turned with a tremulous smile, and he'd swear that she was on the verge of tears.

'I have gin and tonic as you can see, but I would appreciate a glass of iced water. I would prefer not to have a headache in the morning. There will be much to do.'

'Cleaning up, you mean? I'm happy to help out.' He filled a glass with ice and topped it up with bottled water from the fridge.

'Thank you, Dylan. Yes, cleaning up after tonight, but mainly for me, I have guests booked into the day spa all day.' Her hand shook as she lifted the glass to her lips. She tilted her head and her pretty hair fell forward hiding her expression. 'It's good of you to offer, and to help out tonight and let Nat have some time at the wedding. I hear that the casual barman didn't get here.'

'Yes, he missed the boat apparently, but it's all good. I'm happy to help out.'

Sienna lifted her head and held his gaze and her eyes were sad. 'You'll fit in well here. Everyone helps wherever it's needed. What do you think of the island so far?' She had a soft voice and her words were slightly accented.

'I'm very impressed.' He put his hands behind him and leaned back on the opposite counter. 'Everything seems to run well. It's going to be quite a big place when all the new buildings are finished. How long are you here for?'

Stupid question, man. Sounds like you're interested.

'I'm on a working visa, but I'd like to stay here for as long as I can.' She dropped her head again. 'Maybe.'

'From Italy? I'm trying to pick your accent.'

There was no harm in being friendly.

'No. Switzerland. Lucerne. My family are still there in the house I grew up in. On the lake.'

'Really? I did some work in Lucerne before I went to Cornwall.'

She put her glass down on the bar. 'So you've travelled?'

'Yes, my work has taken me to a few countries, but I'm happy to be home in Australia.' He lifted his arms and gestured to the water and the forest. 'And what a beautiful setting to do my work in.'

'Maybe you'd do it better if you'd stop talking and get me a drink.'

Dylan turned and fought a scowl. It was the woman he'd been watching before, the one he'd had to stop on the path this afternoon. He could feel his temper building and that was way out of character; it took a lot to get him cross. Siobhan had told him that was half his problem. He could still hear her voice now.

'You're nothing but a big teddy bear, Dylan. And that gets boring. If you'd been more of a man like Tommy, we wouldn't have ended up like this.'

Like this? Divorced less than a year after his wedding when his wife decided she'd rather live with the best man than the groom. A wedding that had been nothing like this one.

'Hello? I said perhaps you could get me a drink.' The woman spread her hands and her shoulders lifted in an eloquent shrug. 'Looks like you make a better security guard than you do a barman. I can't see Rafe giving you a job on his island.'

Dylan kept his expression bland. 'What would you like to drink, madam?'

Her eyes narrowed, obviously at his lack of reaction.

What a piece of work.

'Are you able to make a cocktail?' She turned to Sienna before he could answer. 'Nothing worse than drinking alone, is there? Will you join me?'

'Just one.' Sienna's smile was sweet, and Dylan thought what a contrast there was between the two women.

'So, Mr Jack-of-all-Trades, do you know how to make a Cosmopolitan?' Her fingers tapped impatiently on the bar.

'If there's cranberry juice in the fridge, I can accommodate that, madam,' he said politely. The time working in bars when he was at university in Brisbane had taught him his cocktails.

'I'm impressed. With your knowledge, not to mention your vocabulary, I thought I'd have you there.' With a dismissive glance, she turned to Sienna and held out her hand. 'Hello, I'm Rafe's friend, Odessa. Where do you fit into this wedding?'

Sienna looked ill-at-ease, but she smiled. 'I'm Sienna. Like Dylan here, I'm an employee. Long story, short: I came here to visit my friend, Eliza—that's her dancing with the guy in the white jacket, he's Phillipe—Pippa offered me a job in *Hebe*, the day spa.'

'Oh, a day spa. I must come and book an appointment,' Odessa said.

'How long will you be here?' Sienna asked. 'The resort fills up again from tomorrow, I believe.'

Dylan could hear the bored tone in Odessa's voice, but her reply dismayed him. 'Oh, I'm here for a month or two, unfortunately.'

If she had to say "unfortunately", why didn't she just go back to where she came from, he wondered. The ruder she got, the more "la-de-da" her accent sounded.

'Why unfortunately?' Sienna asked with a frown.

Dylan's ears pricked up as he opened the fridge and spotted a bottle of cranberry juice. Along with two limes he carried it to the chopping board beside the sink, and deftly sliced the limes. He kept listening as he pulled down two cocktail glasses, the vodka and he scanned the shelf for Cointreau. The bottle was at the far end, and he was aware that Odessa was still watching him as she spoke. Her voice was very cultured, and she enunciated each word slowly. Very different to the tirade of words he'd copped from her earlier.

'Oh, my parents thought I needed a break, so they organised for me to come over to Rafe.'

Lucky Pippa, Dylan thought.

'A break from your job?' Sienna asked. 'What do you do?'

As Dylan turned with the two cocktails, he noticed the colour stain Odessa's cheekbones.

'No, a break from my normal.' Her reply was enigmatic, and she didn't elaborate. Odessa picked up the cocktail he had placed in front of them and she held it up to Sienna's glass. 'So, here's cheers and it really is nice to meet you.'

Dylan was pleased when a group of guests came to the other end of the bar to order, and he was kept busy with a couple of beers, a bottle of wine and another Cosmopolitan. Once he had filled the orders, they went back to the tables and only two men remained.

The taller man held his hand out across the counter. 'Hey there, You're the new landscaper, I hear. I'm Renzo Riccardo—it's my company that's doing the building works. I'd like to sit down and go over some plans with you in the next few days. There's a couple of trees up on the hill where we're pegging out the site, but I think we can work around them, if you think they're worth keeping.'

'What kind of trees are they?' Dylan glanced to the other end of the bar but the two women were in a conversation and had barely touched their cocktails.

'Just a couple of hoop pines, but they're two of the biggest on the island, and the first that you see as you approach the island from the west. I haven't had a chance to talk to Pippa about it yet, but I thought I'd get your advice first.'

'I think I know the two you mean. I've been for a walk up that hill. Where the staff housing is going to be built?'

'Yep, that's right.'

Dylan felt in his pocket, but he didn't have a business card on him. 'Next time you're over on the island let Nell know and she can give me a message.'

Renzo chuckled. 'We'll be back tomorrow.' He gestured to the guy beside him. 'This is Danny, my brother. He's my right hand man.'

Dylan shook Danny's hand, but he seemed preoccupied. He was staring over to where Sienna and Odessa were still talking.

'Danny.' Renzo's voice held a note of warning. 'Take the wine over to the girls while I chat to Dylan. I think Rowena is waiting for a dance.'

Dylan looked across to the table the two men had left. A plump woman with curly black hair sat back glaring over towards the bar, her arms folded. Her voluptuous breasts were almost spilling out of the top of a very tight low-cut red dress.

'When I finish my beer.' Danny picked up his glass and drained it in one hit, his gaze heading immediately back to Odessa and Sienna.

Dylan wondered if he was going to have to go into security mode as he caught Sienna looking over, and then she frowned at the attention the younger guy was giving her.

He'd never been in a place where there were so many undercurrents. Shame, because on the whole it was a happy wedding, and he hoped that none of this tension boiled over into an ugly scene.

'Danny.' This time Renzo's tone held more authority, and Danny shrugged, deferred to his older brother's request, put his glass down and went back to their table.

'Women,' Renzo said, and shook his head. 'You can't live with 'em, and you can't live without 'em.'

I can live quite well without them, Dylan thought, but he gave a non-committal nod, and glanced back at Sienna. She was watching the young builder as he held his hand out, inviting the woman in the red dress to dance.

Sienna's lips were slightly parted in a smile until the woman took Danny's hand and they moved to the dance floor. Dylan's gaze shifted to Odessa and he was surprised to see her watching him. She lifted her glass, and he wasn't sure what she meant.

He moved closer. 'Would you like another cocktail?' he asked politely.

'No, I was raising my glass to thank you. It's an excellent Cosmopolitan.'

'I'm pleased it meets your standards. I'm sure you've been to some very good cocktail bars.' Dylan's words were polite but all he received in return was an eyebrow raise while she sipped, keeping her eyes on him.

He moved to pick up the cloth to wipe the countertop, but she stopped him. 'Wait. Look, I'm sorry I was rude to you this afternoon. I hadn't realised that Rafe had asked that the path be kept clear.'

He nodded, and wiped the counter.

'I thought you were security. But Sienna just told me you're the gardener.'

'Gardener? I'm the landscape architect, yes,' he said not impressed with her tone. Obviously wherever she came from, a security man or a gardener didn't make the grade.

'Well, whatever you are. I'm sorry I was rude.'

'Apology accepted. I was doing my job, so it's no big deal.' Despite his words, he did appreciate the apology. Maybe she wasn't as much of a bitch as she'd first seemed.

'If you're the landscape architect, why are you working the bar tonight?' she fired another question, and he thought he caught a sense of sarcasm.

He raised his eyebrow and briefly considered telling her it was none of her business, but the gentleman in him won. It was hard; it had been a while since he's encountered anyone like her.

'I'm helping out.'

'Paid overtime?'

'No. Now if you've finished with the twenty questions, I have some customers waiting.'

There was a break in the music, and a small group of guests had gathered at the end of the bar closest to the dance floor. Dylan began to fill the orders. When he next looked to the other end of the bar, there were two empty cocktail glasses and two vacant stools. He looked around the restaurant, but there was no sign of the two women.

With a shrug, he picked up the cloth and wiped down the spotless counter top. Despite the snarky Odessa he was enjoying the bar work. If they needed anyone to fill in occasionally, he'd be happy to step in.

Chapter 13

Odessa

One thing Odessa had found with female friendship as she'd navigated her teens and then her twenties, was that alcohol always loosened tongues quickly, and let the establishment of a friendship bypass the usual social niceties and the getting to know you process.

None of the "what school did you go to", or "what does your father do", but straight to "why are you looking so pissed off, let's have another drink" stage.

That was the case with Sienna. As soon as that Italian guy gave her the eye and then asked the gross woman in the skin-tight dress to dance with him, Sienna's mood had plummeted.

'Can I buy you another drink?' Odessa asked, one eye still on the good-looking gardener.

'No, thanks,' Sienna said. 'I think I'll go for a walk down to the bay. It'll be a while before Rafe and Pippa leave, and I won't be missed anyway.'

'You're sounding very sorry for yourself. Want some company?'

'That would be very welcome if you would like to come for a walk.'

They both kicked their shoes off before they stepped onto the sand, and then walked along the shore towards the jetty. The water shimmered silver from the waxing moon above, and a fairyland of lights glimmered in the bay.

'What are those lights?' Odessa asked.

'Sailing boats. Some of the yachties are regulars in the bar. We didn't see them tonight because there was a temporary bar open on the veranda of the house where the guests were served dinner.'

'So, there's often different people here?'

'Oh yes. Between the guests, and the yachties, and the builders and their crew, there are people coming and going all the time. Pippa's talking about opening up the day spa to day visitors soon, but she has to see if Jiminy can bring them over before she starts advertising.'

'What's Pippa like?' Odessa took a step closer to the water and went to paddle her feet.

'Stop.' Sienna's call was shrill. 'Don't go in the water.

Odessa jumped.

'Why not? I'm used to cold water. I'm English, remember?'

Sienna took her arm and guided her back up the sand. 'I know you are, and I'm Swiss, and I'd never heard of stingers and box jelly fish and Irukandji. Plus there can be crocodiles too. That's why we don't go in the water here.'

'What? I'd heard about snakes and spiders but not those other things. They're out here in the ocean? They swim?'

Sienna chuckled. 'They do.'

'And they are really dangerous?'

'Deadly. That's all you need to know. In the daytime you'll see the warning signs Pippa's put on the beach.'

'So,' Odessa said thoughtfully. 'If I go for a swim or put my feet in the water, I could end up dead.'

'There's always a risk of being stung, yes.'

Odessa filed that fact away to think about later.

'Apparently it's worse in the summer,' Sienna continued. 'It might be low risk but it's always there. I haven't seen any crocodiles. I think they're more on the mainland from what I've heard. But if you get hot and want a swim or a snorkel there are stinger suits you can wear.'

'Sounds wonderful.' Odessa pulled a face. 'Not.'

Sienna laughed again. 'Don't worry, there's a pool going in soon.'

'I won't be here that long. And I'm not much of a swimmer anyway.'

'I'm not either.' Sienna was quiet as they strolled along to the jetty where the boat had delivered Odessa and her parents to the resort.

'You didn't answer my question about Pippa. What's she like?' Odessa persisted.

'She's a fabulous boss. She's handed over the day spa to me to manage how I want. She trusts me, and she knew nothing about me, apart from Eliza's recommendation.'

'As a person?'

Sienna shot her an intense look. 'That sounds more than curiosity to me. I can't really comment as we all have different opinions of people.'

'So you don't like her.'

The small flare of satisfaction was soon gone.

'Oh no. Don't get me wrong. She's a lovely person. Good and kind, and a fabulous boss. Everyone loves Pippa. I'm sure you will too.'

'We'll see,' Odessa said drily. 'Okay, so tell me why you looked so upset at the bar?'

Sienna lifted her head quickly and stared at her. She stopped walking and sighed. 'Oh no, was I that obvious?'

'Obvious that you were mooning over that chap? Yes, my sweet, it was obvious to me—and to our perceptive gardener who doesn't seem to miss a trick. He looked quite concerned too.'

Odessa followed Sienna as she took the steps up to the jetty and walked to the end. Sienna sat on the edge of the jetty staring out over the water.

Odessa took a deep breath; the air was clean and pure, and the only sound was the soft sigh of the waves and the occasional call of an unfamiliar bird. As much as she hadn't wanted to come across to the other side of the world, she was beginning to think it might have been what she needed. It was very different to what she'd expected, and quite pleasant.

She sat beside Sienna. 'So?'

'Danny and I have been talking a lot over the past few weeks. I really like him, and I guess when I heard he and his brother were coming to the wedding, I got my hopes up.'

'How?'

Sienna shrugged. 'I guess I was daydreaming a bit. All the other girls on the island have got partners now and I don't want to feel like . . . what's the word? Blueberry? That's what Eliza said when I said she didn't want me around when she met Rocco.'

'You mean gooseberry, and who's Rocco?' Odessa asked with a frown. 'I thought her partner was Phillipe. I can't keep track of everyone here, it must be jet lag.'

Sienna shook her head. 'It is Phillipe. Rocco was Eliza's husband. I still feel guilty that I didn't stop her marrying Rocco. We were together in Florence on a holiday when she met him.'

'So they're not together now.'

'No. He's dead. It's not a nice story.'

Odessa swallowed.

Dead. Like Hannah and Charlie. The darkness swirled in her chest again, rose up into her throat and she knew that she had to breathe evenly to get her breath past that hard lump in her throat. She didn't speak, but she clenched her fists against her sides and focused on her breathing. Maybe she would faint and fall into the water and let it close over her head.

'Anyway,' Sienna said, not noticing Odessa's distress. 'I was hoping to dance with Danny tonight, but I had no idea he was bringing a partner to the wedding with him.' She let out a soft sigh. 'I was reading too much into our talks. The last two weeks he put the finishing touches on the day spa and we talked a lot. He lived in Italy for a while before he started his building trade with his brother. I just really liked him, and I was reading too much into him talking to me.'

The music coming from the restaurant stopped and Sienna pushed herself to her feet gracefully.

'We'd better go back. Pippa and Rafe will probably leave soon.'

'Where are they going? I haven't even had a chance to talk to Rafe yet,' Odessa managed to say. The lump was easing but the darkness was still there.

'They're going to stay on the island for a few months until the building work is done and then I think they plan on going to England for the northern summer.'

Odessa nodded as Sienna waited for her. She turned and looked up at her. 'You go back. I'll stay here for a while. It's very soothing looking out over the water.'

'Are you sure?'

'Yes. I'll be fine.' Her breath hitched again, and she was aware of

Sienna's curiosity as she stared down at her. 'Go on, I'll be fine. Really.'

'Okay, I'll see you back there.'

When Odessa was sure Sienna had gone, she lay back on the wooden planks and stared up at the sky. The stars were brighter than she had ever seen them in the city. The velvet black sky over the ocean was not tainted by light pollution. Thousands upon thousands of pinpricks of light twinkled above her, and made her feel very, very small in the universe.

Her presence on the planet was insignificant. Really, who would miss her, apart from her parents, if she wasn't here?

If she had been in the back seat instead of Charlie, her parents would have grieved, but they would have got over it.

The counsellor at the hospital in London told her that what she was feeling was called survivor guilt. Every day she reassured her that it would pass and gave Odessa strategies to deal with it. *Time heals* was her quiet mantra.

She had to hold onto that thought when these dark feelings took hold of her. She would get over it, she had to; she couldn't spend the rest of her life feeling like this.

The accident hadn't been her fault; in her mind Odessa knew that, but emotionally she had to convince herself that it wasn't her fault.

But it was hard.

So bloody hard.

Too bloody hard.

Chapter 14

Pippa

Today, our wedding day, had been the most wonderful day of my life. The lack of any family there for me didn't take away from the joy; the presence of my friends had made up for that. We danced and laughed and enjoyed celebrating with people we loved and loved us in return.

We'd cut the wedding cake—an incredible concoction that Cherry had created. Cherry was our trainee chef, and partner of Angus, who was taking over as head chef now that Tamsin was pregnant.

I stood and stretched as Rafe went over to the bar to get a glass of water for me—I was determined not to be hungover from my wedding, I didn't want to miss one minute of it by drinking too much.

Jiminy, my friend from high school, who was now bringing the resort guests over on his boat, stood beside me. He put his arm around my waist and his lips brushed my cheek.

'Congratulations, Pippa. You look gorgeous. Sarah and I are really happy for both of you. You don't look anything like that wild schoolgirl who used to get the boat across to school with me all those years ago.'

'A lot's happened since then,' I said.

Jiminy nodded and looked around. 'Whoever would have thought that this resort would be on your Aunty Vi's island. God, she'd be proud of you, Pip.'

'She would be happy, wouldn't she? She'd be out on the dance floor dancing nonstop if she was still with us. She sure knew how to have fun.' I looked up as Rafe joined us and passed me a glass of iced water.

'Pippa, would you mind if I asked Odessa to dance? Just a quick one?' Rafe looked across at Jiminy and put on a mock-stern face. 'There is duty to be done.'

'You are a true gentleman, Rafe,' Jiminy said as Rafe looked at me with his eyebrows raised.

'Of course I don't mind. Go ahead,' I assured him.

'Dance with me, Pippa? If you want to, that is.' Jiminy's cheeks flushed red.

'Oh, yes.' I grinned at him as Rafe left us. 'I'll step on your toes and pay you back for all those times you pulled my braids on the bus when we were at high school.'

'I never did,' he said indignantly and then grinned back at me. 'Not more than once anyway.' Jiminy held his arms wide and I stepped into them.

The music swelled as Jiminy led me onto the dance floor and I was surprised by how well he danced. We did two circuits of the small floor passing Rafe and Odessa each time.

'Shocked you, didn't I? Thought I was a boatie who knew nothing else,' he said with a cheeky grin. 'Sarah made me do ballroom dancing before our wedding.'

'Ha ha. Now why would I think that? And good on Sarah. Who's minding the kids tonight? I'm sorry we couldn't invite them.' My words were all over the place as I tried, and failed, to focus on our conversation. I really didn't want to see Rafe dancing with his English friend. I could just imagine the gloating expression on her face if she saw me looking. In the end I couldn't help myself, but strangely, I felt sorry for her when I glanced across the dance floor. She held my eye for a brief moment, and there was no gloating there, just sadness.

'Don't be sorry.' Jiminy's voice pulled me back. 'A wedding's no place for kids. Besides, they were quite happy to see us leave this afternoon. Sarah's parents came over from Airlie Beach, and the kids will be spoiled rotten tonight. New toys, eat whatever they want, and stay up watching movies all night.'

'Sounds good to me.' I kept my eyes on Jiminy's when I heard Rafe talking to Odessa near us. 'Nothing like grandparents to spoil them,' I said.

There was a break in the music before the chorus began, and the words that I heard Rafe say were imprinted on my mind. 'No, Odessa. I'm sorry. I cannot and I will not.'

Before I could hear any more, the volume increased and Jiminy twirled me across the dance floor.

##

Could not what? I wondered.

I quickly got over my brief surge of jealousy and a glass of wine helped me chill. Rafe sitting close to me with his arm loosely around my shoulder as we talked to Tam and Gabe, and Nell and Nat, helped.

There was no sign of Odessa, and I noticed Sienna had disappeared too. I'd kept an eye out for her earlier because she was sitting by herself after the dinner. She'd sat at the table with Eliza and Phillipe, and Evie and Jed while the meal was served, but she hadn't looked happy. I don't know what was wrong because she'd been fine when she and Evie had helped me get ready for the wedding.

I looked up as I heard chairs being moved. Eliza and Phillipe, and Evie and

Jed were joining our table and we all moved along to fit them in.

Eliza squeezed into the space on my left. 'Happy?'

'I am,' I replied.

'The ceremony was beautiful, and the dinner was amazing.'

'The meal was incredible,' I said. 'Angus excelled himself. I told the kitchen staff to call in for a drink when they finished, but I think they've all gone back to the house.'

'They have. They're over there having a few staff drinks on the veranda. They didn't want to impose on the wedding.'

'Oh, that was thoughtful, but they would have been welcome.'

I looked around the restaurant again. Small groups of guests were sitting together talking. Catherine, the wedding celebrant, was deep in conversation with Jenny and Bryant, and loud laughter carried across from the table where the Riccardos were sitting. Jiminy and Sarah were the only ones left on the dance floor and seemed oblivious to anyone else. There was still no sign of Sienna.

'Where's Sienna gone?' I asked with a frown. 'I noticed she looked a bit lost earlier.'

'She's palled up with Rafe's friend. I think they've gone for a walk down to the beach together.'

'Odessa?'

'Yes.'

'Oh,' I said.

Eliza's eyes narrowed. 'Oh, what?'

'I'm surprised, that's all.' I kept my voice low. 'I just didn't think she seemed very friendly.'

'Really? We had a good chat before. She seems nice, but I don't know how impressed she is with the island. I think she might get bored here.'

I shrugged. 'We'll see.'

The next hour passed very happily as Rafe and I moved around and talked to everyone, thanking them for coming. Renzo and Danny Riccardo both grabbed me, and each took a turn to hold me in a tight hug. I smiled as they both kissed Rafe on each cheek. A lot of back slapping, laughter and congratulations came our way.

Renzo introduced me to his wife, Maria, but Danny seemed to be ignoring the woman beside him. She was staring into her wine and didn't acknowledge either of us.

As we walked back to the table where we had been sitting, Jiminy called us over.

'How much longer do you want us to stay, Pip?' he asked. 'I was thinking about rounding up those who are heading back to Hamo shortly.' He glanced down at his watch. 'I got a shock when I saw what time it was. The night's gone quickly. Shows what a great time we've all had. I've danced with Sarah so much tonight I've got brownie points for weeks.' He put his arm around his wife, and she shook her head.

'You just lost them all, boyo.'

Jiminy chuckled. 'See what you've got ahead of you, Rafe?'

Rafe chuckled and I couldn't hold back the yawn that had been threatening for a while.

'I think it's time we left too,' Rafe said. 'Jim, grab the microphone and let them all know the boat will be going in what? Say, half an hour?'

'Sounds good.' Jiminy did as Rafe asked.

Our group of island friends over at the big table—with the exception of

Tamsin—looked as though they'd settled in for the night. Her head was on Gabe's shoulder and her eyelids were drooping.

I glanced over at the bar. Dylan was still there, wiping down and polishing glasses—he was a good worker. I honestly hadn't seen him stop moving since he'd arrived on the island.

'Excuse me for a minute,' I said and headed to the bar. 'Dylan, thanks so much for helping out tonight. I think you've done most of the night by yourself. We really appreciated you stepping in.'

'It was my pleasure, Pippa,' he said. His full lips lifted in a smile, and his dark eyes crinkled at the edges. He was a fine looking man. Tall and strong, but he exuded a quiet and gentle manner. I liked him.

'Well, thank you, again, and make sure you take a day off tomorrow.'

'I'm going to go for a walk up to the peak,' he said.

'Enjoy yourself.'

Jenny and Bryant were standing beside Rafe when I came back. 'We're heading to bed now,' Jenny said. 'Jet lag has finally kicked in.'

'You've done well to last this late,' Rafe said. He pulled Jenny in for a hug. 'I'm so pleased you all decided to come.'

'*We're* so pleased,' I corrected him as I hugged Jenny and then kissed Bryant's cheek. 'I'm looking forward to getting to know you both. Rafe speaks so affectionately of his time with you.' I grinned at Jenny. 'You know, Jenny, the first night I saw Rafe on Hamilton Island—before I knew he was the difficult man who owned half of my island—'

'Hey,' my husband interrupted. 'You owned half my island.'

I ignored him. 'Anyway, Jenny. Rafe was with you that night in the restaurant. Never in a trillion years did I dream that I'd meet you at our wedding a year later.'

'It was meant to be, Pippa,' she said as she hugged me back. 'And I'm looking forward to getting to know you too.'

'We'll see you both tomorrow,' Rafe said. 'But it won't be early. I think we all need a sleep in.'

His words elicited some risqué comments from the table where our friends were. I rolled my eyes.

'Come on Pip, it's your wedding night. We have to tease you,' Tamsin called out.

'Last time I looked you were asleep on Gabe's shoulder,' I said with a laugh. 'Okay, tease away, you lot. My husband and I are going to bed now. But feel free to party on. Nat, you'll have to get their drinks. I told Dylan to knock off. He's been great.'

Rafe's arm went around my shoulder, and I snuggled in.

'Come on, wife, Let's go home.' He held me close as we walked along the beach and headed towards our home up on the hill.

Our first night as a married couple.

I held his hand tightly as we walked up the steps and joy filled me. The emptiness that I had carried for such a long time was gone; it had been filled by Rafe's love. Gradually at first, and then as I learned to trust, it filled the emptiness within me in one huge rush.

We didn't speak. Words weren't necessary.

Rafe opened the gate that led to the small garden on the cliffside of our home, and stopped. I let out a contented sigh as his arms went around me and gentle lips sought mine.

My lips opened beneath his and my husband kissed me for a long time, before he murmured against my mouth.

'Are you ready to be carried over the threshold, Mrs Rendell?'

'You might tear my dress,' I said shaking my head.

'That can be remedied.'

I laughed as his fingers searched and finally found the concealed zipper on the side of my dress. Slowly he lowered it, and as I lifted my arms the moonlight bathed my bare skin in a translucent glow.

Rafe carefully folded my wedding dress, and handed it to me before he scooped me into his arms and carried me towards our home.

Chapter 15

Dylan

The last two days had been full on and being on his feet in the bar for a few hours had added to Dylan's tiredness. He took a quick shower in the small bathroom near his room, and crashed into bed, sleep overtaking him immediately.

It only seemed like moments later when a loud constant knocking woke him. He lay there for a moment, but the noise continued. It seemed to be coming from the back of the house across the lawn.

Quickly pulling on a pair of jeans over his boxers, he closed the door behind him. He hurried across to the entrance of the small building and, as he pushed the outside door open, the knocking got louder.

An outside security light bathed the Englishman who was knocking on the back door of the house. His wife stood on the bottom step below him.

Dylan called out as he crossed the lawn. 'Hello, is everything all right?'

The woman—Jenny, Dylan recalled her name—put one hand to her chest, as her husband turned.

'Thank you, we couldn't raise anyone, and the door is locked,' he said.

'What's wrong?' Dylan asked. 'Are you locked out of your hut?'

Before the man could answer, the door opened and Tamsin came down the two steps to join them on the lawn.

'What's happened? Bryant, what's wrong?' she asked.

'We can't find Odessa.' Jenny's voice trembled.

'What do you mean you can't find her? Where have you looked?' Tamsin asked.

'After we left the restaurant just after midnight we went back to our hut and made a cup of tea. We sat and talked for about an hour,' Bryant said.

'Even though we were tired, we couldn't get to sleep because we haven't adjusted to the new time yet,' Jenny said. 'When we finished, I went to check on . . . to say goodnight to Odessa but she didn't answer. I went back to our hut, but I couldn't stop worrying, could I, Bry?'

'No.' Her husband reached for her hand. 'I went to the hut and knocked. When she didn't answer I opened the door, and she wasn't there.'

'We thought she left the wedding early and went to bed. She was tired from the long trip, plus her medication makes her tired anyway.'

Tamsin shook her head. 'She went for a walk with Sienna after dinner and I haven't seen either of them since they left the bar.'

'Where have you looked?' Dylan asked.

'The hut, the path to the beach, and as far as the jetty. We also went back to the restaurant, but it was in darkness.'

'Yes, we turned everything off and came to bed not long after you left.'

'We might seem as though we are overreacting,' Bryant's forehead creased in a frown, 'but Odessa hasn't been well, so we're more concerned than perhaps seems normal.'

'We didn't want to bother Rafe and Pippa, that would have been inappropriate on their wedding night,' Jenny said. 'So we came here to see if anyone could suggest where we should look, or what we should do. It's so isolated here.'

Dylan took charge. 'I'm guessing that everyone is in a pretty deep sleep in there,' he said to Tamsin, gesturing to the house.

'Yes, most of them had a few drinks. I wouldn't like to see them on the bush tracks tonight. We'd end up with a few lost out there.'

'Where are the bush tracks?' Jenny's words were high pitched, and Dylan could see she was close to panic mode. 'Where do they go to?'

'Tamsin—' Before he could finish, Dylan was interrupted.

'I can help.'

Dylan hadn't noticed Angus join them. 'Thanks, mate. Tamsin,' he continued, 'you go and see if Sienna is in her room, and then Angus and I will go out looking. Jenny and Bryant, you stay here. It's dark out there, and the paths are quite dangerous as you head up towards Red Wave Wall. If Sienna is with Odessa, and they went that far, there's a good chance that they weren't game to come down in the dark. The track goes close to the cliff edge.'

'Thank you.' Jenny took a deep breath and put a hand on Dylan's arm. 'I'm so sorry to cause this bother on our first day here.'

'Don't be silly. It's not your doing,' Tamsin said. 'I'll go and check if Sienna's back. Wait here.'

As Tamsin went into the house, Bryant put both arms around Jenny and she rested her head on his shoulder.

Dylan turned to Angus and gestured for him to move away from the couple with him as he spoke quietly. 'Have you had much to drink, mate?'

The chef shook his head. 'No, just one beer. Listen, Cherry's awake too, and she only had a Coke. If we have to go out looking, we'd be better to work in pairs. It's pretty hairy up that hill.'

'I've heard that. A favourite of rock climbers,' Dylan said. 'I haven't been up there. I intended climbing the peak tomorrow.'

'Yeah, Cherry and I walked as far as Red Wave Wall last week. There's feral goats up there too.'

The door opened and Tamsin hurried down the steps closely followed by Sienna.

Jenny drew in a loud breath. 'You're here.'

Sienna's eyes were wide. 'I'm so sorry. I left Odessa out on the jetty. She wanted to look at the stars a bit longer. I was . . . tired. I said I was going back to the restaurant but I changed my mind and came straight here and went to bed.' Sienna put her head down and looked a bit embarrassed. 'I should have gone back to the restaurant, but I knew Pippa would understand.'

Dylan frowned. "Understand" was a strange choice of word.

'It's all right, love. It's not your fault.' Jenny moved away from Bryant and reached out and touched Sienna's arm. 'Was she all right? Did she seem upset?'

Sienna shook her head. 'No, she was fine. We talked about not being able to swim in the bay, and'—she tipped her head to the side—'we talked about the island, and working here. She asked me what Pippa was like.'

Jenny and Bryant exchanged a glance and then Jenny kept firing questions. 'Did she intend coming back to the restaurant? Did she say what she was going to do. She's walked a lot since . . .'

Sienna put her hand to her face. 'I don't think she did, but I really can't remember. She was looking at the stars. I do remember she said she hadn't had much of a chance to talk to Rafe, so I guess I just assumed she'd head back to the wedding and talk to Rafe and Pippa.'

'Okay.' Dylan took control. 'Now that we know that, we need to co-ordinate what we're going to do. I was in the local volunteer search and rescue group when I was in Cornwall, and I've had experience in many searches.' He turned to Jenny. 'Look, the conditions are perfect here. A warm night and no rain. I'm sure she'll be fine.' He didn't voice his worry of drownings or falling off cliff faces. 'I'll get my phone and we can exchange numbers and that way, if she comes back, you can let us know. Angus, go grab your phone and put some sturdy shoes on. Same for Cherry, if she's happy to come with us.'

Jenny nodded, her face pale.

Dylan ran back to his room, pulled a T-shirt over his head, and grabbed his walking shoes and a pair of socks before he picked up his phone. He'd put it on the charger when he'd gone to bed and the battery was almost at full capacity.

When he returned, Angus was back with Cherry, and Gabe was there too.

'Cherry's coming with me,' Angus said.

'I'll come too. I didn't have much to drink tonight. Last night, I mean. It's after two a.m.' Gabe looked at Tamsin. 'You take Jenny and Bryant to the kitchen in the house and put some coffee on.'

'I was going to help search,' Tamsin protested. Dylan saw the look that passed between them and finally she nodded.

'Okay. Kitchen it is.' She reached up and kissed Gabe. 'You be careful, it's dark out there now that the moon's set.'

Dylan exchanged phone numbers with Bryant and Angus, and then Tamsin took the older couple to the kitchen.

'Would you prefer coffee or tea?' she asked as they walked up the stairs.

'Tea please,' Bryant said.

'We're English, after all,' Jenny said lightly but her voice hitched in a sob.

Sienna spoke quietly. 'I'd like to come and search too.'

'Okay,' Dylan said. 'You pair up with Gabe. If you two follow the shoreline from the house to the far rocks, and check the jetty, I'll head up the track. Angus and Cherry, if you could check all the paths through the rainforest, and then take the one that goes over to the bay on the other side of the island, that should cover most of where she could have walked to.'

'Right,' Angus said.

'If you find her, send a text to all of us. Did you get all the phone numbers?'

Gabe and Angus nodded, and Angus and Cherry headed off.

Dylan had a quiet word to Gabe while Sienna went to get a pair of boots. 'Keep an eye in the water. I hate to think the worst, but if she fell off that jetty . . . '

'Or worse,' Gabe said quietly. 'Tam told me that Odessa has come over here to get over some problems.'

Dylan nodded. That made sense. Both her interactions with him had been intense and he'd sensed that she had been worked up about something. Rafe had managed to settle her down on the path when she'd been insisting on finding Pippa, and when they had talked at the bar, her eyes had glittered hard and bright, and her manner had been insulting, sarcastic and dismissive despite her apology.

Dylan had met women like that before, but despite that, he'd still found himself watching her during the evening. She was a very beautiful woman, and when she wasn't trying to put on an act, she had an air of vulnerability about her. He knew what it was like to be unhappy, and he sensed that was what lay beneath her brash and cocky behaviour.

And now she was missing, and who knew what she was capable of.

Sienna ran lightly down the stairs. She now wore a pair of jeans, a long sleeved T-shirt and sturdy boots.

'I'll walk with you two until the path turns off to the peak,' Dylan said as he turned on the flashlight app on his phone. 'I wish we had some good lights.'

'It's less than two hours until first light,' Gabe said.

'True,' Dylan replied. 'I still haven't acclimatised to being back in Australia.'

'How long have you been back?' Sienna asked.

'I arrived from the UK two days before I came to Pentecost Island. I couldn't face another winter over there, and my contract was up, so I decided to come home.'

They reached the point where the path diverged, and Sienna grabbed Dylan's hand. 'I do hope we find her quickly. I feel guilty. If I'd stayed with Odessa and we'd walked back together, we wouldn't be wandering around in the dark looking for her now.'

'It's not your fault, and I'm sure it'll be fine.' Dylan tried to reassure her. Sienna had looked upset at the wedding as it was, without blaming herself for Odessa disappearing. 'I'll text you when I get to the top of the path,' he said. 'I'm sure she'll turn up quickly. It's only a small island.'

Dylan headed into the rainforest, and Sienna and Gabe walked the path that led to the beach.

Chapter 16

Odessa

Odessa had stayed on the jetty for a long time after Sienna went back to the wedding. The music started up again and as she focused her thoughts, the music drifting down from the restaurant faded into the background. Gradually the blackness had lifted, and she made herself breathe deeply as Jemima, the psychologist, had taught her.

She had been a kind woman and obviously good at her job, but even though Odessa had listened to what she had said, she had barely spoken to the woman.

Ask yourself who is truly responsible, she'd told her. If she considered that, it had been Hannah and her lack of confidence driving on the motorway.

'Dealing with the sadness and grief is the hardest,' Jemima had said. 'It might sound harsh but focusing on guilt is often a way to avoid that. In a week or two I want you to think about the intense emotion that you are experiencing, Odessa.' Jemima had put her small hand on her arm and Odessa had stared at it. 'We all process grief in different ways. Some of us internalise, and some of us scream and yell, and that's okay. Whatever works for you is okay.'

Her parents didn't know she'd stopped taking her anti-depressant medication two weeks ago. Maybe it had been the wrong decision, but that's what she'd wanted to do.

But it was hard.

Oh, God it was so hard.

Jemima had told her to find something positive to focus on. Her thoughts kept returning to Hannah's family.

Hannah's grandmother, Vivian, had come to see her when she was in the hospital. She'd held Odessa close, but she hadn't cried. Her shoulders straight and her voice steady, she had been stoic, and had talked to Odessa for two hours.

Before she left, Vivian had lifted her head and her graceful neck seemed to be more wrinkled than it had at the birthday party. 'I can be strong, darling, and I want you to be strong too. There has been a waste of two lives. Don't let your grief burden you down. I want you to promise me that you will do something with your life.' She'd held Odessa's hands so tightly it had hurt and her eyes had held hers for a full minute before she spoke again.

'My darling Hannah has gone, and you were spared. Don't waste that gift.'

In that moment, Odessa had vowed to follow her dream of making jewellery and the first pieces she made would be something for Hannah's mother and Vivian that would be a link to Hannah.

As much as she hadn't wanted to come to Pentecost Island, these few weeks would be a chance for her to regroup, recover and start planning how she would do that. Jemima had told her that, most importantly, she had to look after herself physically.

'Eat well, and sleep well, and your body will help your spirit recover, Odessa. It will take a few months, but in time you will make sense of it all.'

Maybe she would, but right now she was having trouble making sense of anything. Maybe it was the jet lag that was making her feel worse.

As Odessa walked along the jetty, she couldn't bear the thought of going back to the wedding. It was Rafe's day, and he'd chosen a wife who would now keep him here. She had to accept that her special friendship with Rafe was over, and she wouldn't see him as much as she had before he moved to Australia.

And even if Odessa didn't particularly like his wife, she knew Pippa was his choice and his life. He was part of a new group of people now and just because she was here, she didn't have to be part of that close-knit group.

It seemed no different to what she'd left behind.

And she wasn't going to waste her time like that ever again.

Odessa had intended going back to the wedding, but as she'd walked along the path, the laughter and happiness met her like a huge crushing wave, and she knew she couldn't go back there.

Indecision filled her; she was wide awake, and she didn't want to go back to the hut.

With determined steps, she turned away from the restaurant and took another path.

##

Dylan

The first part of the path wound through a dense pocket of rainforest and the leaf mulch crunched beneath Dylan's boots. A couple of times he heard creatures scurry away on the path ahead of him. He flashed his phone to the left and the right scanning the bush as he made his way along the path. Possums and rats he could deal with, but he wasn't too fussed on stepping on a snake or walking face-first into a spiderweb.

Dratted woman, he thought uncharitably as a wave of tiredness rolled over him. He'd been sleeping soundly when the knocking had woken him, and if there was one thing Dylan needed it was his eight hours sleep each night.

He wondered if he should be calling out her name, but instinct told him if she was up here, she may not want to be found. He moved as quietly as he could as the path began to ascend.

After ten minutes of a fairly steep climb, and he was beginning to puff, he reached what he first thought was the top of the hill. But looking ahead, he realised it was a false crest and he was only halfway to the top. The moon had set, and the slight wind had dropped away. The side of the island and the mountain ahead were in darkness, and the mournful horn of a ship echoed across the water. An ominous feeling prickled his neck.

She could be anywhere. It was hopeless.

Dylan paused on the flat area of rock-strewn dirt and caught his breath. He took the opportunity to flash his phone ahead, but there was no sign of anyone. A faint sound caught his attention and he cocked his head to the side and listened. It had sounded like a faint cry, but as he stood there, a flutter of wings stirred the air, and the cry was repeated as a bird dipped below the side of the hill, its mournful call hanging on the night air.

Below him he could see two pinpricks of light as Gabe and Sienna, and Angus and Cherry made their way along the beach paths and through the forest. The lights would bob for an instant and then disappear as they headed into thicker bush.

He took a deep breath and set off up the hill again, and as the path narrowed he used the flashlight on his phone more frequently to guide his way. After a couple of hundred metres, the path was barely a track, and Dylan could smell the salt tang of the sea below. He flashed his light and stepped back, shocked.

The edge of the path was less than a metre from him and beyond, a sheer cliff plunged a couple of hundred metres down to the sea. Taking a deep breath he stood and looked out over the water. To the east, a smidgeon of pink stained the sky heralding the dawn.

Despite the dangerous drop it was a beautiful sight, and he thought how spectacular it would be in full daylight. Setting off again, this time he kept the flashlight on ahead of him and kept well to the right side of the path away from the cliff edge. He shivered as he thought how close he'd gone to the edge without knowing. God forbid, Odessa had come this way in the dark.

The only sound was the one persistent, and obviously distressed, bird that kept flying over him, swooping down to the water and then soaring above the track again to return moments later. There were no trees nearby. Perhaps there was a nest on the ground that she was protecting.

After another ten minutes of climbing, Dylan spotted a fork in the track ahead and thought back to when he'd studied the map the other day. From memory, the path to the right led to the peak, the high volcanic cone that made Pentecost Island so unique and beautiful, and the path to the left led to Red Wave Wall, the escarpment that was a popular rock-climbing destination.

Dylan stood there for a moment and thought, pondering his choices. No one in their right mind would attempt to climb that towering peak in pitch darkness and without proper climbing gear. There was no way Odessa would have gone that way.

He hoped.

Huffing a breath, he took the left fork and as the path widened and moved away from the cliff edge, he strode along. Suddenly, ahead of him, he heard footsteps and the rattle of stones.

'Odessa,' he called urgently, quickening his pace. He held the phone up and the flashlight illuminated the path ahead.

'Shit,' he mouthed with disappointment as a lone goat scampered up the almost sheer rock wall ahead. He'd reached the end of the track and above him was the sheer face of Red Wave Wall.

Dylan pulled out his phone and sent a group message to those searching and waiting below.

Reached the end of the track. No sign of her. On way down. Any luck down there?

Three messages came straight back. All negative.

With a sigh, he switched his phone off. Two hours wasted and no sign of Odessa. The bad feeling stayed in his chest; he'd been involved in search and rescues where the outcome had been tragic, and this was not looking good. It was a strange time to go missing in the middle of the night on an island she had only arrived on and wasn't familiar with.

At least the sky was lighter now, and he knew what to expect on the track as he descended. Dylan turned and headed back towards the resort.

When he reached the fork where the path split, he stopped for a rest and to consider their options. He guessed once it was morning and Pippa and Rafe were informed that Odessa was missing—if she hadn't turned up by then—the police would be called and watercraft brought in to search. Maybe a helicopter. His volunteer search and rescue work had only started since he'd been in the UK and he was unsure of the local processes here; he only knew what he'd seen on news programs.

The sky was getting lighter and he could see the silhouette of a flat rock at the edge of the path away from the cliff's edge. As he walked across, the soft rose pink at the edge of the horizon deepened into apricot, and he knew dawn was not far off. The dawn of an unpleasant day that would take the happiness from Pippa and Rafe's wedding.

Maybe if he'd kept talking to Odessa at the bar last night, she wouldn't have wandered away. Her sarcasm had bugged him; he'd had enough of that from Siobhan to do him a lifetime.

Dylan turned to face the sea again and leaned back on the rock, his thoughts churning. The island was small, but there would be so many places she could be.

'Find your own rock,' came a sarcastic voice from the other side of the rock. 'I was here first.'

'Jaysus, Mary and Joseph, what the hell are you doing here?' Dylan jumped as Odessa pushed herself to her feet on the other side of the rock.

'I was tempted to stop you and ask the same thing when you strolled past me around three a.m.'

Chapter 17

Dylan

As he watched in disbelief, the woman he'd been searching for stood and moved to his side of the flat rock. She was still wearing her green dress, but her hair was now loose and covering her shoulders.

Relief flooded through him, but it was tainted with anger as he pulled his phone out. 'What? Are you telling me you were here all the time? You were here when I walked through here on my way up to that blasted wall?' He lowered the hand holding the phone, unable to take in the fact that she'd been behind this rock and he'd walked right past her, and she hadn't let him know she was there.

Not a word.

He'd climbed what seemed like another ten bloody thousand feet when he could have been tucked up in his bed.

'What's it to you where I've been? I chose not to give away my presence behind this rock. I was enjoying the solitude.'

'Enjoying the friggin' solitude! At three o'clock in the morning? Do you realise the whole island is being searched for you as we stand here and have this ridiculous conversation?' Dylan stood and gaped like a fish as she protested.

'Oh bugger! Did Mummy go to check on me in my bed? They drive me crazy, you know. I am not a child or a wild teenager on a curfew. I've been almost engaged three times, and I live in my own apartment. Honestly, they are hopeless.'

His anger grew as her laughter surrounded him and his fingers stabbed into the keys of his phone.

Found her. She's fine. We'll be back soon.

'What are you doing?' she said moving closer to him. A waft of musky—and he was sure, expensive—perfume drifted over him, and his anger exploded.

'What am I doing? I'm telling people who care about you that you're not bloody dead. Do you know what you've put your parents through tonight? How selfish and inconsiderate you are? Do you know there are people who worked hard all day to make yesterday a success who have given up their sleep to look for you?'

She drew herself up straight and stepped closer so that her face was right in his. Her words were cultured and precise. She had the hide of a bull elephant, and Dylan decided in that moment that he really didn't like her one bit.

'I called you a gorilla the other day, and I wasn't far wrong, was I? If I want to go for a walk and wait to see the sun rise, that, sir, is none of your business. Or my parents, or anyone else's, for that matter.'

Dylan held his tongue because he knew if he spoke, he'd regret the words that came out. He'd already said more than he should have.

Her tone lowered to a placatory level. 'Look it's all a fuss in a teacup. I am perfectly fine, and if it wasn't for my mother thinking I'm suicidal every time I take some time out, no one would be going without sleep. Now I'd be really grateful if you would disappear down that path, and leave me to enjoy my solitude and the sunrise.'

'No. You can come down with me.'

'I will do no such thing.'

'You will.' He stood in front of her and folded his arms.

'I won't.' She folded her arms.

'Well, then, I guess madam will just have to put up with my company until she sees the sunrise and then decides to come down.'

'It's a free world. You can do what you want. But if you do decide to stay up here, please don't talk to me. I've heard enough of your opinions to do me for a lifetime.'

Dylan pulled out his phone and lifted it. 'Smile please.'

'What the hell?'

'I'm going to explain that you are going to watch the sunrise. If your parents see you are all right, they'll go to bed and stop worrying.'

'Oh, you are such a kind and thoughtful gorilla. Take my photo, send your bloody message and then piss off.'

Before Dylan could take the photo, her eyes widened, and he was surprised when she put a shaking hand up to her face. For a moment he thought she was fixing her hair for the photo.

He waited until she lowered her hand and he clicked the photo.

'Now if I ask you politely, will you please go and leave me in peace? Please?' Her voice broke on the "please" and she lifted her hand again and this time it was to wipe her eyes.

Dylan's eyes narrowed; she wasn't as calm as she'd been making out, and the suicidal comment that she'd made stayed with him. He had thought she looked vulnerable when he'd watched her last night.

He lowered his voice and spoke gently. 'Look, let's start over. I apologise for interrupting your solitude, and I'm very sorry that I lost my temper.' He forced a grin. 'I'm usually quite a gentle gorilla, you know. You seem to bring out the worst in me.'

'Oh I'm good at that. I can bring out the worst in most people without even trying.' Bitterness laced her words. 'And it often has a very unhappy ending. I'm not a very nice person, you see, Dylan, so you really don't want to be around me.'

He stared at her and wondered what had happened to make her so bitter. He kept his voice low. 'I'd like to stay and watch the sunrise too. Especially after that climb. I'm quite happy to keep to my side of the rock, and I promise I won't break into song or rave on about the beauty of nature. I can enjoy it quietly.'

'Send that photo to my parents and they can go to bed.'

He quickly sent the photo with a short text.

All good. Staying up here to watch the sun rise. Go to bed.

She stared at him warily as he put the phone back in his pocket. and gestured to the edge of the cliff. 'I know what you're thinking and why you want to stay.' Her tone held a tiredness that obviously went bone deep. 'Look, yes, I have been depressed, and yes, I know what people are saying about me, but I came here to get away from all that. I just want to be left in peace. Can't anyone understand that. I need time and I need space. Please—'

Dylan was dismayed when Odessa suddenly bent over and put her hands over her face. A high keening wail that made goose bumps raise on his skin came from her lips. He moved to her instinctively and put his arms around her. Holding her close he was surprised by the frailty of her body against him. She was tiny; he hadn't realised just how thin she was.

***

Odessa

Odessa was horrified when she lost control, but no matter how hard she tried to compose herself, she couldn't stop crying. She sobbed and ranted as a torrent of words flowed from her lips that were pressed against a hard shoulder. Firm hands held her close; if Dylan hadn't held her, she knew she would have fallen.

Ever since she'd left the hospital, she'd held her emotions in check; it had been easy when she had taken the medication that the doctor had insisted she continue for six months.

No matter how hard it would get, she knew she needed to be able to feel and not control and subdue her emotions with drugs if she was ever going to get over the horror of the accident. When she came out of hospital, her parents had insisted that she move in with them, and that had been her first mistake. Having her every move and every word watched and analysed had put her in a place where she'd merely said what was expected and behaved accordingly. Pretending that everything was normal had resulted in a great mass of emotion staying inside and getting darker and stronger every day.

She was tired of being watched every minute of the day, as her parents seemed to expect some awful breakdown.

Well, she'd just had it.

The freedom of walking up that hill in the middle of the night had loosened that tension within her. The words she'd exchanged with her rescuer—or rather her unexpected sympathetic companion—had breached the tight control she'd held since she'd flushed the medication down the toilet.

It was the first time Odessa had let her emotions out since the first day in the hospital after the accident. As her sobbing lessened, she realised her rescuer was holding her close, and his large hands were rubbing soothing circles on her back.

He didn't speak, and she started talking, and taking gulps of air between sobs and words.

'If I had made Hannah let me drive . . . if I'd been in the back . . .oh, poor Charlie . . . Vivian will be disappointed in me . . . and now I can't talk to Rafe anymore . . . and I know his wife hates me . . . I hate me.' She dragged in another huge gulp of air, and those gentle hands patted and soothed. 'I didn't want to come here. But I'm here and . . . I have to do something for Vivian . . . I don't know what to do.' She lifted her face away from his shoulder and didn't care that her eyes were red, and her nose streaming. 'Dylan, please help me. Tell me what I should do,' she whispered.

Her back felt bare and cold when he lifted his hands, but they moved to her shoulders and he held her in a firm but gentle grip.

'I suggest what we both do is move a little bit to the left where there is a small patch of grass and we can lean against that rock and watch the sun rise, without thinking about anything apart from how beautiful it's going to be. Then we can talk. If you want to. How does that sound?'

She nodded mutely and let him lead her to the grassy spot next to the rock. Her breath hitched as she realised that it was the place that she'd sat a couple of hours ago, but she had frightened herself when she kept looking at the drop below and moved back behind the rock. Maybe her mother was right. Maybe her thoughts had gone in that direction when the guilt had almost crushed her.

She'd been on the grass when she'd heard someone coming up the hill. At first, she'd been frightened, worrying that it was a wild creature of some sort, but as he'd come closer, he'd flicked a light on and shone it ahead and she'd realised it was him.

Not wanting to reveal her presence or explain herself to anyone, Odessa had pressed against the rock, and he'd walked right past. She knew he'd come back but hadn't been prepared for him to stop right beside her in the dark on his way down.

Once they were seated with the rock behind them, Dylan's arm went around her and she put her head on his shoulder. She felt drained and her eyelids were heavy.

'Thank you, I—really—'

'Sssh. Just relax.'

Odessa closed her eyes and listened to the quiet breathing of the man holding her. Her first impression of Dylan had been wrong; he certainly wasn't the gorilla she'd accused him of being. He was kind and gentle. Most men of her acquaintance would have left her up here, if she'd talked to them like that.

Except for dear Charlie.

Her breath hitched again. Odessa tensed and sniffed as tears threatened; Charlie would have stayed with her.

The hand resting on her arm moved up and down in a soothing motion.

'Sssh, Dylan said. 'Don't think. Just enjoy the quiet. Close your eyes and I'll tell you when the sun is about to rise.'

Odessa snuggled into his side. 'You're a nice man, Dylan. If you want to sing when the sun rises I won't complain.' Her eyes closed and sleep overtook her.

Chapter 18

Pippa

In that delicious moment between sleep and waking I turned my face into the soft feather pillow and an unfamiliar floral fragrance tickled my nose. I inhaled slowly and stretched my legs out against the cool Egyptian cotton sheets. They were soft against my bare skin, and I thought about going back to sleep. I wrinkled my nose and opened my eyes; it was the pillowcase that held the unusual sweet smell.

'I love watching you wake up.' Rafe's deep voice had me opening my eyes wide.

'Hair spray,' I said.

'Hair spray? That's a strange morning greeting for your new husband. Perhaps you're not awake yet,' Rafe teased as he bent down to kiss me. 'I need coffee and I was trying not to wake you.'

'It's hairspray. I can smell it on the pillow from my hairdo yesterday.' I reached up and put my arms around his neck. 'There's no need to get up yet. It's only early, isn't it?' I looked across to the window and realised that the blinds were down and that was why the room was dark.

'It's after ten. We slept very late.'

'I guess I'd better get up then. Back to work today.'

'Yes, it is. And I'd like to go down and spend some time with Jenny and Bryant. They're only staying on the island for four days.'

'What about Odessa? She didn't seem to spend much time at the wedding last night.'

'Jenny said she went for a rest but she did come back for the meal. Anyway, I can spend some time with

Odessa when they leave.' My husband of less than one day smoothed his hand gently over my hair and then cupped my cheek. 'You won't mind, will you, love?'

'No, of course I don't mind.'

And I meant it. Yesterday Rafe and I had promised our hearts and lives to each other, and I trusted him implicitly. 'She's been through an awful experience. Rafe, I know what loss is like, and I know how it affected me for a long time when my parents died.' Rafe knew the story of my father's death in an oil rig accident and my mother's suicide the same year.

'I'm worried about her. She seemed to be very much on the edge of breaking last night. I'd love you to get to know the Odessa of old. She was vibrant, full of life and nothing ever worried her.'

'What did she do? For a job, I mean? Was she in the family publishing company too?'

'No. She didn't do anything as far as I know.'

'No job? Uni?' I asked.

'No. I'll go and put the coffee on and then tell you more.' Rafe leaned over and his lips brushed mine.

I put one hand behind his head and held him close.

'Are you sure you want to get out of bed?' I asked with a provocative smile.

'I don't, but don't you have a meeting with Renzo this morning?' He grinned. 'I told you to take Sunday off and now you know why.'

'Oh, damn,' I said letting go of him and sitting up quickly. 'Yes, he had to come over this morning because he has to fly to Brisbane this afternoon for business for the week. He'd got a few projects on the go around the state. We're taking a final look at the site for the staff accommodation at eleven before they start excavating.'

'He and his wife should have stayed the night.'

'They could have, but Maria said they had to get back because the babysitter couldn't stay. What time did you say it was now?'

'A quarter past ten.'

'How about you put the coffee on and then come and keep me company in the shower. I have to wash my hair.' I slowly ran my fingers down Rafe's bare chest, stopping at the top of his boxer shorts.

'Ah, I've married myself a wanton wench,' he said as he climbed out of the bed. He paused in the doorway. 'But I do love her.'

##

Thirty minutes later I stood on our balcony sipping the coffee that Rafe had brewed. The sun was shining, and the water of the Whitsunday Passage was its usual brilliant blue. Being Sunday the water was dotted with more sails than usual as local residents took advantage of the perfect spring weather. Happiness filled me as I looked down over our resort; it was growing so quickly.

'Yesterday was perfect, wasn't it?' Rafe said as he came outside to join me.

'It was. I think everyone had a good time. I wonder how long it'll be before the next wedding. Gabe and Tam are engaged, and Nat and Nell look very cosy together.'

Rafe chuckled. 'Leave them be. Now that you're a married woman, you want everyone else to follow suit. Come on, we'll have to walk down now unless you want to be late for Renzo.'

I put my cup on the table and Rafe held the gate open for me, and then took my hand as we headed down the path. 'The only one I was worried about last night was Sienna. She seemed a bit . . . I don't know . . . distracted. She wasn't her usual outgoing self.'

'I noticed that too,' Rafe said. 'She was quiet. Although I was pleased to see her sitting and talking with Odessa for a while.'

'I'll ask Eliza if Sienna's okay. I do hope she's not getting homesick just as we're ready to get the spa going.'

When we reached the path at the bottom of the hill, Rafe stopped and pulled me into his arms. 'Do you know why Ma Carmichael's is going so well?'

I looked around. 'Because it's in such a wonderful setting and we have good people on board.'

'No, it's you, Phillipa. And I don't want you to ever doubt it. It's your dream that's being realised, and it's happening so well because of you. Because of the person you are. You care about your friends and you care about the staff you didn't know. You put people first, and that's the special ingredient that is making this place go so well.'

A warm glow filled me as he held my gaze.

'Thank you. That means a lot to me.'

He raised my hand to his lips and as we headed towards the restaurant where I'd organised to meet Renzo, happy voices and laughter greeted us.

Chapter 19

Odessa

'Odessa.' The quiet deep voice saying her name belonged to the man in her dream. 'Wake up.'

Odessa opened her eyes and blinked as the soft cotton of a T-shirt rubbed against her nose. Dylan was still holding her close, and she assumed he had been since they had sat down on the grass.

'The sun's about to rise. I thought you wouldn't want to miss it, seeing you climbed all the way up here to see it.'

Odessa sat up, rubbed her eyes and then ran her fingers through her hair. Her voice was husky as she turned to Dylan. 'I went to sleep.'

'You did. And you've been asleep for almost an hour.'

'Thank you,' she said quietly, looking out to sea. She was too embarrassed to meet his gaze. 'I had a bit of a meltdown, didn't I?'

'Do you feel better for it?' he asked quietly.

She bit her lip and then nodded. 'I do.' The constant pressure that had been in her chest was gone.

Dylan pushed himself to his feet and held his hand out. She slid her hand into his and let him pull her up to her feet.

They stood quietly together, and she slowly let go of his hand. The first curved sliver of gold peeked above the horizon, and a low bank of cumulonimbus cloud above was edged with a deep pink rim. Odessa drew a breath as the huge golden orb slowly rose until it seemed to hover above the dark blue water before beginning its climb into the sky as the new day dawned.

'Oh my God,' she whispered. 'I have never seen anything more beautiful in my entire life.'

'Magnificent, wasn't it? I'm really happy to be living on Pentecost Island. It's a pretty special place,' Dylan said. 'Look at the colour of the mountains on the mainland.' He gently took her shoulders and turned her to face the west. In the far distance the tops of the mountains glowed gold and the gullies were shadowed in dark green.

'The colours are so strong. Breathtaking. At home, we have soft green fields and a watery blue sky.'

'I know. I've lived over there for the past two years.'

'I heard you telling Sienna last night you were in Cornwall.' She put her head down. 'When I was being particularly rude to you. I'm sorry. My behaviour has been awful.'

He looked at her curiously. 'Is it okay if I ask why? I sort of picked up before that you had something bad happen in your life. If you'd rather not talk about it . . .'

She held his gaze. 'I think I do need to talk about it. I've avoided talking for the past eight weeks, and it's all jammed in me and turned me into this horrible person. Are you sure? It would be a bit of a relief. I mean you don't know me and I can be honest.'

Dylan turned and patted the rock that was beginning to catch the warmth of the tropical sunshine. 'Jump up here next to me and talk to your heart's content and then we'll walk back down, and you can shout me a coffee.'

'I'm sorry.' Odessa bit her lip again. 'You haven't had any sleep, have you? Do you have to work today?'

'No, it's Sunday. I can go back and sleep all day.'

'Where do the staff live?' she asked.

'The girls are in the original house and Angus, the chef and I bunk down in an old building at the back of the house.' He pointed down the hill. 'See the red roof of the old house? If you follow the bush up the hill, there're some new buildings going up there, for the staff. Pippa said when the resort is full-size, there'll be about thirty staff on the island permanently.'

'What's Pippa like?'

'So far I find her very good. I've only been on the island a short time. She's really happy to give me a free hand with the landscaping. I'm imagining something like I did in Cornwall, but with different plants of course. '

'What did you do over there?'

'I was one of the head gardeners at Nancarrow Gardens.'

'I haven't been to Cornwall.' She pulled a face. 'I'm ashamed to say I haven't been far from London. I mean I've travelled extensively in Europe, but I haven't seen much of the UK.'

'I loved it. I did a lot of travelling on weekends when I was in Cornwall. The distances are nothing like Australia.'

'So tell me about Nancarrow Gardens.' Odessa was feeling calm and was genuinely keen to listen. It was the first interest she'd felt in anything since the accident.

'It's a thirty acre garden surrounding Nancarrow Castle in a beautiful Cornish valley.' Dylan's eyes lit up with enthusiasm as he told her about his work. 'There's over four miles of footpaths under canopies that burst with exotic blooms with colours that

I've never seen in plants anywhere else. The paths lead down to the private beach below the castle. It's also got a lot of historical interest. It has its very own Smugglers' Cove.' He chuckled and she looked up and held his gaze. 'It took me back to my Famous Five days.'

She smiled. 'So why did you leave?'

He shrugged. 'Homesick for blue skies and familiar country, I guess. Anyway enough about me. Tell me about you.'

Odessa kept standing, but she leaned back against the rock that Dylan was sitting on. 'I was in a car accident on the way back to London. Two of my friends were killed instantly, and I got out with barely a scratch. I haven't coped well with it.'

'That's understandable,' Dylan said quietly.

'So to cut a long story short, my parents thought it would be a good idea to ship me out to stay here with Rafe to recuperate. They were coming to the wedding anyway, so they made me come.' She knew her laugh was bitter. 'At my age, imagine, doing what your parents tell you. I think it's the first time in my life I ever have. I think they knew that Rafe would be good for me. He was always getting me out of trouble in my late teens.' She looked away from him out over the water. 'I always thought that Rafe would marry me, and then he married his first wife and got divorced, and hey presto, before I knew it, he's married again. So, I guess I've missed that boat.'

***

Dylan

'Are you in love with him?' Dylan waited until Odessa lifted her face and met his eyes again. Her eyes were not red or puffy anymore; they had cleared now and it was hard to tell she'd had a crying jag in his arms before she'd gone to sleep. 'Sorry, maybe that's a bit personal, but if you are, it might be a difficult situation with him only married yesterday.' Dylan knew how complicated relationships could get. Odessa was enough of an emotional mess without unrequited love being factored in.

'No. I love him, but I'm not in love with him. Don't worry, I wouldn't do anything to mess up his life. I couldn't help myself yesterday when you stopped me on the path. I guess I took it upon myself to make sure that Rafe was marrying the right person this time. I'm really sorry I was so rude to you.'

'They seem to be very happy.' Dylan had been slightly envious yesterday when he'd seen how Pippa and Rafe had looked at each other. Siobhan had never looked at him like that, even on their wedding day. 'I'd hate to see anything cause them grief,' he said carefully.

'I'll be on my best behaviour. I don't know Pippa, but I'll do nothing to hurt Rafe.'

He must have looked uncertain, because she reached for his hand and squeezed it. 'I promise. Trust me.'

He nodded and gestured down the hill. 'We should probably head off before they send out another search party.'

'Dylan?' Odessa tipped her head to the side and he thought again how beautiful she was.

'Yes?' He cleared his throat and looked away. He had no intention of getting involved with another woman.

'Can I ask that you keep this to ourselves. My parents worry about me enough without knowing I had a full-blown meltdown on a mountain in the middle of the night.'

'My lips are sealed,' he said. 'I stayed up here with you because I wanted to see the sun rise too.'

'Thank you.'

He couldn't help himself. 'If you need an ear again while you're on the island, come and talk to me. You'll find me in one of the gardens or glades. It's not a very big island.'

Odessa looked down past him. 'You can see how small it is from here. I didn't think I was going to like it here, but you know what? I'm going to give it my best shot.'

He held out his hand before they headed down the hill.

It was only because she was wearing flimsy sandals, and the track was steep, he told himself.

Chapter 20

Pippa

I was surprised to see Danny waiting in the restaurant with Renzo when Rafe and I walked in just before eleven. Jenny and Bryant were there having a late breakfast, and four of the tables were filled with guests from the huts. One of the casual kitchen hands had stayed on the island overnight and was running the coffee shop for Cherry. I'd insisted that she and Angus take the day off today. There was no sign of any of the others.

It was time we hired more staff; the problem was, they had to come over from Hamo each day until the staff quarters were built.

'You go and meet with Renzo, and then we'll have lunch with Jenny and

Bryant,' Rafe said. 'Is that okay with you?'

'Of course,' I said as we headed for the table overlooking the water where Jenny and Bryant were sitting. Bryant stood and leaned over and kissed my cheek, and Jenny smiled up at both of us.

'Hi there,' I said. 'I've just got a quick meeting with the builders, and then Rafe suggested we have lunch together.'

'That sounds wonderful,' Jenny said.

'Where's Odessa?' Rafe asked looking around.

Bryant shook his head. 'She's having a sleep in. Would you believe she climbed the mountain this morning so she could see the sunrise!'

'What?' Rafe's eyes widened in horror. 'Not the peak?'

'No, about halfway up.'

'By herself?' I asked. 'There's wild goats up there.'

Jenny and Bryant looked at each other for a moment.

'Ah, she had company,' Bryant said. 'That gardener chap was with her.'

Rafe frowned. 'Dylan?'

'I don't know his name. He walked her back to the hut just as we were going for a walk about eight o'clock. Odessa was animated and raving about the island.'

'That's excellent. Pentecost Island is weaving its magic already by the sound of things,' Pippa said.

Rafe shook his head. 'But I can't get over that she climbed up there to see the sunrise after the wedding. It's not an easy walk.'

'Well, she's sleeping it off now,' Bryant said.

I left them chatting as I made my way across to the Riccardo brothers. Renzo had his laptop out and was typing as he waited for me. Danny—who was usually bright and full of cheek—had his head cradled on one hand as he held a huge coffee in the other.

'Morning, guys,' I said.

'Morning, Pippa.' Renzo was brisk and businesslike as usual, and he snapped his laptop shut as soon as I sat down at the table. 'I asked Danny to come over with me this morning too, because he'll be in charge of the excavating while I'm away this week. No point putting it on hold, is there? There is work to be done and we have a schedule.'

I shook my head. Renzo fired his words out like bullets and sometimes with his Italian accent it was hard to keep up. But I was pleased with their work. We were ahead of schedule by two weeks.

'I want Danny to be very clear about where the building will be located.'

Renzo had drawn up the plans for the staff quarters and a single story lodge that was going to be built on the hill up behind the old house. As well as sixteen small bedrooms, with four large bathrooms, there was a staff kitchen, and a dining room and living area. He'd designed it so that it would blend into the rainforest on the hill, and of course under current building standards, it had to be cyclone safe. Thanks to Eliza coming on board as a financial partner after she had sold her ex—and dead—husband's villa in Tuscany, we were able to move ahead at a fast rate.

I reminded myself that I needed to meet with Dylan to work out how we were going to access it from the resort but make the pathway private. The description of the work—and the photos I'd seen—of the gardens he'd designed in Cornwall had given me some ideas, but I was sure he would have something suitable in mind. We'd been lucky to get him for our small island; he was very qualified and had a raft of experience in Australia and England.

The last thing we wanted was guests wandering up there inadvertently. We were getting an excellent staff group together and I wanted to keep it that way. Providing private and suitable accommodation on the island would hopefully entice more quality workers.

'Hurry up and finish your coffee, Danny,' Renzo said, a tad impatiently, interrupting my flow of thoughts. 'We need to get up that hill. Are you right to go, Pippa?'

'Yes, I'm right. I'd like to be as quick as possible too.'

Renzo stood and pushed his chair in and it scraped on the pavers.

Danny flinched.

I shot a sympathetic glance at him, noticing bloodshot eyes. 'Need a hair of the dog, Dan?' I asked. 'I can order you a bloody Mary.'

'Water will be fine, thanks. I'll grab a bottle from the fridge.' He hurried over and grabbed two bottles. 'Put it on my tab.'

I shook my head. 'As it was my wedding, I feel some responsibility for your hangover.'

'I kept drinking on the boat on the way home. Foolish move,' he said. 'Especially with an early start this morning. But we had a good night, thanks for inviting us.'

I wasn't sure who he was referring to by "us". Danny had pretty well ignored his partner all night as far as I'd noticed as Rafe and I had mingled amongst the guests.

Renzo strode ahead and as Danny and I followed him, laughter from the lawn had me turning my head. The rest of the gang were coming in for breakfast. Evie and Jed were arm in arm, Eliza and Phillipe were deep in conversation, Tamsin and Nell were giggling together, followed by Gabe and Nat. There was no sign of Sienna or Dylan, although I figured if Dylan had been up the mountain, he'd be having a sleep in too. Sienna had mentioned something about guests wanting the day spa today so at a guess, that's where she was.

'I'll be back to see you all in a short while,' I called out.

Waves and smiles followed me as we headed towards the path that led up the hill. We were almost to the forest when we met Sienna hurrying from the old house towards the day spa.

'Morning, can't stop,' she said brightly and kept going. 'Running late for an appointment.'

Danny went to speak to her, but Sienna put her head down and didn't look back. We had almost reached the bottom of the hill when Danny stopped.

'I'll meet you up there. I need to use the bathroom.'

Renzo made a noise that sounded like a disgusted grunt. 'Well, hurry up.'

Danny took off and when I glanced back, I was surprised to see him take the path that led to the day spa.

I followed Renzo up the hill.

Chapter 21

Odessa

Hunger woke Odessa after only a couple of hours sleep. She'd only picked at her meal at the wedding last night, and the walk up the mountain and back down again had taken all her energy. Not to mention the crying jag that filled her with embarrassment when she thought about it.

Dylan had been very kind to her, and she cringed more as she remembered their first meeting. If someone had treated her like that, she would have cut them dead. At least there was someone here she felt comfortable with now. Her parents were watching her like a hawk, and she was sure they'd told Rafe to do the same. Pippa was distant with her and she couldn't blame her, and the others on the island seemed to be such a tight group, she really didn't want to waste time getting to know them all.

God, she'd soaked Dylan's shirt with her tears telling him what she'd been through. Maybe if she'd been that honest with Jemima, she'd be at home and getting back to her life.

She needed to talk to Rafe. That was her focus today.

Odessa's stomach grumbled as she stepped out of the shower and reached for the thick white towel. The quality of the hut and its fittings had surprised her; it was a lot more luxurious than she'd expected. The bed was comfortable, the bathroom was small but beautifully fitted out, and if she was honest, the view from the small porch was as good as anything she'd seen in Europe.

Better actually. Being on the water's edge and watching the colours change the water helped her focus and stay calm. She dried herself and quickly wound her damp hair into a clip. As well as needing food, she didn't want to lie around wasting time; she'd thought about what she was going to do and she intended to get started.

Today.

Odessa had made a plan, and she needed some time with Rafe to set it in motion. She pulled on a white sundress and ignored the pang of grief that shot through her when she remembered it was one she had bought in Harrods that last day shopping with Hannah.

'Block the sadness,' she told herself sternly. 'Remember instead how we laughed and how we had fun that day.'

She headed off towards the restaurant, knowing it was probably too late for breakfast but hoping that she could at least get a coffee. She frowned as she approached the outdoor restaurant and voices and laughter met her. It sounded like there was a crowd there.

The last thing she wanted to do was get involved in conversation. Stopping, she tapped one finger against her lip, tempted to turn around.

Maybe she could go up to Rafe's house?

With another frown she shook her head. No, she wasn't ready to talk to his wife yet.

Irritation threatened to overwhelm her. What a stupid place to live. Really! Who'd choose to live on a tiny island like this.

No shops, no coffee shops. All she wanted was a coffee and something to eat without seeing anybody before she found Rafe.

As Odessa stood there deciding what to do, footsteps approached along the path ahead.

She went to duck into the forest but paused when Dylan appeared ahead.

'Good morning,' he said with a wide smile as he approached her. 'Again.' He looked fresh and bright and had obviously had a shower. Damp hair curled onto his neck.

'Where are you going? I thought you'd be sleeping in on your day off,' she said quietly.

'I'm in search of coffee and food, in that order,' he said.

'Me too,' Odessa admitted. 'But it sounds very crowded over there, and I don't really feel like company yet.'

He stood there and looked down at her without speaking, and she stepped to the side of the path.

'Well, I'll let you go then,' she said.

Dylan shook his head and turned back the way he'd come. 'Come with me. We'll go to the kitchen in the house. That way you won't have to be sociable if you don't want to. Is the company of one suitable? There was no one else there when I walked past.'

'Is that okay?'

'Yes, there's a section at the back of the kitchen for the staff. I can get coffee and rustle us up something to eat.' He laughed, and again Odessa thought what a kind man he was. He was gentle and there was no bluff or bluster about him. Comfortable in his own skin, he obviously didn't see the need to try to impress.

'What do you fancy? I cook a mean French toast.'

'Are you sure?' she asked, and then nodded. 'I love French toast.'

Fifteen minutes later, she was sitting in a big old fashioned kitchen, and Dylan had a pan sizzling on a huge gas range. He'd brewed them both a coffee in the coffee machine in the corner, and now Odessa wrapped her hands around the mug as she watched him cook.

'How many pieces,' he asked as he deftly turned the first one over.

'Oh, only one, thank you.'

He shook his head as he looked over his shoulder at her. 'I beg to differ. Once you taste my cooking, you'll come back for more. Maple syrup or tomato sauce?'

'Um—' Before she could finish speaking, one of the bridesmaids from yesterday walked in from the veranda— the blonde one called Tamsin. Odessa put her head down and stared into her coffee.

'Morning, Dylan,' she said and then looked taken aback when she saw Odessa sitting there. 'Oh hello.' Her tone was cool. 'Back from your adventure?' she said.

Odessa sat straight. 'Adventure?'

'Last night up the mountain. I heard there were a few search parties out there in the wee small hours.

'I'm afraid I don't know about that. I walked up to see the sunrise.' She lifted her chin and stared. 'Is there a law against that on the island?' Odessa knew she was being rude, but the other woman had started it. She wasn't going to be patronised by some Aussie chick who thought she was better than anyone else.

'Fair enough.' The blonde turned to Dylan. 'They're still serving brunch over in the new restaurant. You didn't need to cook your own.' She threw a last curious glance at Odessa. 'Anyway, I just came over for some more eggs from the cool room. They've run out over there. Feeding hangovers, I think.'

'Is Rafe over there too?' Odessa butted in and received another cool considering look.

'Yes, I believe he's having breakfast with your parents.' Her tone made it sound like an accusation as though Odessa should be doing the same and not associating with the staff.

'Thank you. I'll join them after I finish here.'

Tamsin shrugged and disappeared through the door.

Dylan looked at her curiously as he placed a slice of golden crispy bread onto her plate, but he didn't say anything about her being rude again.

Again. Odessa huffed a sigh. She was going to have to try harder.

They ate quietly and when she'd finished, Odessa stood and picked up her plate.

'Leave it, I'll load the dishwasher,' Dylan said.

She nodded and put her plate and mug on the sink. 'Thank you for that, it was delicious. You are a man of many talents. Landscape gardener, psychologist, and excellent cook and cocktail maker.'

Dylan's smile was gentle. 'It's called self-sufficiency.'

'That's what I need to find,' Odessa said. She realised what he'd said. 'You could have been a counsellor. Thank you again for this morning.'

'My pleasure.' Dylan stared past her and seemed briefly distracted. 'I did a lot of reading when I went through a bit of a tough time before I went to the UK. If I was able to help you, I'm pleased.' He stood and brought his plate across to the sink. 'Come on, I'll walk you over to the restaurant and then I'll come back here and clean up.'

'There's no need.' Odessa moved towards the door. 'I can find it.'

'I insist. My mother taught me to be a gentleman.'

She smiled at him. 'She was very successful.'

'Come this way, it's quicker to join the path from the back of the house. He led her down two steps and onto a lush green lawn edged with colourful flowers. A path of pavers led across the lawn to what looked like an extra-large garden shed.

'That's where Angus and I bunk down,' Dylan said. 'There's three small rooms and a bathroom at this end, and you can't see, but it's an L-shape and my workshop is at that end. I don't spend much time in there, it's mainly to store the mowers and tools.'

'A workshop?' Odessa's interest was piqued. And you don't use it?'

'No, I'm either out on the island working, and when I plan, I use my computer in the loungeroom of the old house.'

'I haven't been able to get internet on my laptop here,' Odessa said. 'Is there any Wi-Fi on the island?'

Dylan nodded. 'I know Pippa's been talking to Nat—he's Nell, the office manager's partner and he and Gabe work in IT together. At the moment you can pick up a strong signal in the house here, because it faces Hamilton Island where the tower is, and there's a booster in the outside bar.' He chuckled. 'I think she is going to extend it to the huts, but at the moment, the guests go up to the bar.'

'Good for business there, I guess,' Odessa said. 'They buy drinks while they browse. I'll head up there later then.'

'If you'd rather come over here where it's quieter, I'll be working here this afternoon. I have some plans to draw up.'

'It's okay. I'll need to spend some time with my parents, I guess. But thank you.'

Dylan walked with her as far as a small glade near the restaurant. 'I'll leave you here. I hope you have a good day.'

Odessa couldn't help herself. She stood on her tiptoes and brushed a light kiss on his cheek. 'Thank you for being so kind to me.'

She turned and headed towards the noise and laughter.

Chapter 22

Dylan

Dylan was thoughtful as he walked back to the house. He'd enjoyed Odessa's company—even though she'd been prickly to Tamsin—but he didn't want her to get the wrong idea. The kiss—albeit on his cheek—had been a warning for him to pull back. He knew from what she'd said that she was going to stay for a couple of months on the island, and the last thing he wanted was to give her the wrong idea.

Odessa was an interesting character—not to mention beautiful—and he'd found himself drawn to her more than he should be.

Dylan reminded himself why he'd come to the island. He'd wanted to come back to Australia, and one of the reasons he'd applied for this position was because there was no chance of running into Siobhan and Tommy. If he'd gone back to Brisbane, he would have done eventually as they shared the same group of friends. Last he'd heard Siobhan was pregnant with their second child; she and Tommy hadn't wasted much time.

He turned off the path before he reached the house and walked down to the beach. Listening to Odessa and comforting her on the mountain had brought back many of the feelings he'd had when his marriage had broken down.

If you could call someone meeting you at the door on the way home from work with a packed suitcase a marriage breakdown.

He'd had no idea that Siobhan had been seeing someone else, and when she'd left and then the divorce papers arrived a few weeks later, he'd been devastated.

Even more so, when he'd found out it was his best mate—and best man at the wedding, Tommy Hammond.

Dylan walked across and sat on the flat rock looking over the Whitsunday Passage. He hadn't really known Siobhan; and he still had no idea why she had married him.

If the truth be known, he shouldn't have proposed. He'd known that she'd manipulated him into it, but he'd been—or he thought he'd been— in love with the person that he'd thought she was. Six months of living with her had shown him that he'd made a mistake, but Dylan had been prepared to work on it.

His self-confidence had taken a hit, and he'd applied for—and thankfully been successful in winning—the job in Cornwall. He'd taken some time to travel around Europe before he'd started. The two years there had healed him; the divorce had been finalised quickly and he'd moved on, immersing himself in his work.

There was no way he was going to let another woman manipulate him; he had a feeling that Odessa could be dangerous to his peace of mind.

***

Odessa

Odessa stepped out of the rainforest at the edge of the outdoor bar at the same time that Pippa walked in from a path that came down from the small hill. She swallowed, determined to be polite. Being with Dylan had been calming.

'Good morning, Pippa,' she said brightly.

She waited while Pippa walked across the lawn to join her and Odessa saw her hesitation before she smiled back.

'You're up early. Your parents said you climbed the mountain to see the sun rise. It's spectacular, isn't it?'

'Pentecost Island is spectacular. And what you've done with the accommodation is beautiful.'

'Thank you. And welcome to our island. With the wedding and all that happened yesterday, I didn't get a chance to tell you how happy we are to have you here as a guest.'

Odessa hid a smile at the "we". Pippa was making it very clear that Rafe was hers, and that she was here as a guest and not a friend.

'Thank you, I'm looking forward to my time here. Would you mind if I have a quick private word to Rafe before we join the group?'

'Of course not. Why should I mind?' There was a defensiveness in Pippa's tone.

Odessa didn't reply. What could she say?

As they reached the restaurant, Rafe looked up and smiled, but his smile was for Pippa first.

Pippa left Odessa and walked across to the table where a large group of their friends were sitting. Odessa still hadn't worked out who was staff and who were friends. Uncertainty rippled through her and then she spotted her parents at the far end of the table. She headed over, but Rafe met her on the lawn when she was almost there.

'Good morning.' He reached down and brushed his lips across her cheek. 'Pippa said you wanted a word? Is everything okay?' His stare was intense. 'Are you okay?'

'I am. Your island is working its magic. I feel the best I have since . . . since the accident. I wanted to talk to you about an idea I have.'

'Of course.' Rafe led her over to the bar and pulled out one of the high stools. 'It's a bit quieter over here. I think that lot are still on a high from the wedding.' He smiled as they both looked over to the table where the laughter seemed to be nonstop. 'Then again it's like that here most of the time.' He gestured to the coffee bar. 'I'll get you a coffee. And what would you like to eat?'

She held up her hand. 'I've already eaten, thank you. Sit down, this won't take long.'

Chapter 23

Pippa

I tried not to let the little green monster niggle too much when Rafe and Odessa put their heads together and talked for a good half hour. They had known each other for a long time and they were friends. I had to remember that. The problem was I felt as though I was walking on eggshells whenever she was mentioned.

The same with Rafe. His voice was reserved when she came up in conversation. Maybe it would get easier when she'd been here a while.

And maybe it'll get worse, a little voice chirped in my head. Jenny and Bryant had gone back to their hut, and Renzo was waiting for Danny to reappear. He and Danny had come over in Renzo's motorboat, and he had looked around exasperated when Danny didn't come back.

'*Inaffidabile e pigro*,' Renzo muttered as he'd looked at his watch.

'Pardon?' I said.

He jumped to his feet. 'Please tell my *unreliable* and *lazy* little brother that he can get the launch back with Jiminy later. There's plenty for him to do here. He can start pegging out the building on the hill. I can't wait any longer.'

'Okay, have a good week, Renzo. And thanks for coming over on a Sunday. I'll see you when you get back.' I was thoughtful as I watched him stride down to the beach and head towards the jetty. I suspected that Danny had gone to see Sienna, and that worried me because she's looked upset when he'd had a partner with him at the wedding last night.

'Hey, girl, what are you looking so worried about the day after your wedding?' Tam had moved to the chair that Renzo had vacated.

I smiled at her. 'Absolutely nothing. Happy as.'

'So why the frown before?' Tam nodded towards the bar where Rafe and Odessa were still sitting close. 'Madam giving you sass too?'

'What do you mean too?' I burred up. Odessa could treat me however she liked, but she could treat my friends and the resort guests with respect.

'She has attitude,' Tam said folding her arms. 'Although it might have been because I interrupted a cosy brekky she was having with Dylan.'

'Where? Here? I thought she'd just surfaced.'

'No, over at the house.'

'She shouldn't have been there; it's not open for guests today.'

'I got the impression she was there with Dylan. He was cooking French toast for her.'

'Fair enough.' I shrugged. 'That's his call. And I suppose she's not technically a guest. She's Rafe's visitor. She's here to get better.'

Tam tipped her head to the side. 'You said yesterday she'd had a tragedy. Are we allowed to know what happened? Maybe I'll be a little bit more forgiving.'

'I suppose so. But let me check with Rafe first. I'd hate her to think I was gossiping about her.'

'She makes you uncomfortable, doesn't she, Pip?'

'A little, I guess, if I'm honest. It's a part of Rafe's life that I wasn't aware of, and it unsettles me a little bit. *She* unsettles me, but I've got to show some empathy.'

Tam reached over and gave me a quick hug.

'Well you know where to come if you need to talk. Now, I think a mimosa is on order to celebrate your first day of being married.' With a giggle she put her fingers up and clicked them as Nat headed for the bar.

'*Garçon, s'il vous plaît,*' she said in such an awful French accent, Phillipe rolled his eyes and Eliza giggled. 'Another round of mimosas for the girls, please. Oh and look here comes, Sienna, just in time.'

I turned to see Sienna walking up along the beach, and she looked happier. Maybe it was because Danny was walking beside her.

Maybe I needed to have a talk to her too.

But first I was going to relax and enjoy a pleasant Sunday. The first Sunday of my married life.

By the time I had a glass of champagne and orange juice in front of me and was chatting to Nell, Rafe was sitting beside me again and there was no sign of Odessa.

He put his arm around the back of my chair and I smiled up at him.

'Everything okay?' I asked.

'Yes, really good. Odessa is happy and I can see a change in her already. She's going to start work as soon as she can, and she had a suggestion, but I said I'd have to run it by you first.'

'What sort of work? Don't tell me she wants to be a waitress?'

'God, no. I can't see Odessa in a kitchen, can you?'

'To be honest? No.'

'It's all come from a talk she had with Hannah's grandmother about doing something worthwhile. Hannah was one of the friends who was killed in the accident. Odessa has always wanted to pursue a career in jewellery making, and she's asked if she could use a bench in the building at the back of the old house. She works with silver and she's going online to order all her supplies later today, and get them delivered here. She wants to talk to you about it when she comes back with her laptop later. Is that okay with you?' His voice was guarded.

'What, that I talk to her, or that she does it?'

'Both, I guess.'

'I can't see a problem. As long as it's away from the guests, and Dylan and Angus don't mind.'

'Thanks, love. I think having a focus is going to make a huge difference. She's quite excited about the idea.'

I shrugged. 'Whatever we can do to help.'

Chapter 24

Four days later

Dylan

Dylan wasn't sure how he felt about Odessa moving into the building. Pippa had come to see him on Sunday and had run Odessa's requests by him.

Requests.

He wasn't bothered by her working at a bench in the workshop; he barely spent any time in there, but he wasn't so sure about her moving into the spare bedroom at the back of the building.

He'd decided after breakfast on Sunday that he was way too interested in her, and that he'd be keeping his distance from now on. After all, she was a guest, and he was staff, he'd be working on the resort so there was really no need to see her.

'It's up to you, Dylan,' Pippa had said. 'But as Odessa pointed out, she's going to be on the island for a couple of months and staying there will free up one of the huts. I offered for her to stay with Rafe and I up at the house, but she said that wasn't fair to us.'

'That was very thoughtful of her. Pippa, I don't see any problem, apart from her having to share the bathroom with two blokes. Did you talk to Angus?'

'No need to.' Pippa's grin widened. 'The girls have all done a swap around. Cherry is taking one of the bigger bedrooms in the house—the one that Evie and Jed have been in— and Angus is going to share with her. Talk about an island of happy ever afters,' she said. 'Watch out you could be next.'

'No fear of that,' he said. 'I've tried that, and it didn't work for me.'

'I'm sorry to hear that,' Pippa said.

'Yep, married once. And that will do me for a lifetime. I'm here to make Pentecost Island one of the top tropical gardens in Queensland.'

'If that's your focus, I'm certainly not going to complain.'

'Look, I don't have a problem with her moving in. It'll give her a chance to get to know the girls better too. I'm sure Odessa and I won't see much of each other anyway. I'll be putting in some long hours over the summer.'

'Thanks, Dylan, I appreciate your co-operation. She'll spend the rest of the week in the hut, and then move over on Friday after her parents leave.'

#

It would have been a lot easier doing that week if Odessa had kept her distance. At least once each day, she would encounter him wherever he was working, and by the third day, when he changed his plans, so he was in a more isolated part of the forest, she still managed to 'stumble' upon him on one of her walks.

The problem was that Dylan enjoyed the daily visits and chats, and on the fourth day Odessa brought him a snack from the bar and a cold drink.

'I could get used to this,' he said as he sat beside her on one of the seats in the glade that Evie had created on the way up to the mountain.

'I hope you don't mind me seeking you out,' she said with a smile.

'No. I enjoy the company. How's your research going?' Odessa had told him that she was about to begin silversmithing in the workshop.

'Excellent. I've ordered the first of my supplies from Mackay, and they should come by express post any day.'

'That's great news.' Dylan put his drink down on the ground beside him and held her gaze. 'And how are you going? Are you feeling a bit more settled?'

She looked away from him, but she nodded. 'I am. It's amazing how the beauty of this place seeps into your soul. The only thing I'm a bit hesitant about is my parents leaving tomorrow. I know I've ordered those supplies, but I still wonder if I should go back with them.'

'I thought you were here for a while.'

'I am, but I'm a bit of a misfit on the island. The friendship group is so strong, I feel like I'm back at boarding school and not part of the "in" group.'

'I'm sure they don't mean to make you feel like that. They're all really nice women. I'd say it's because everything's back to normal and they're all busy.'

'Sienna's busy, but she still finds time to be pleasant to me. And as much as I enjoy spending time with Rafe, that's not fair on Pippa. I don't know why they didn't go away somewhere.'

Dylan changed the subject, because he had noticed that Odessa wasn't readily included, and he felt awkward discussing his employers with her. Maybe things would get better when she moved into the staff accommodation tomorrow.

'If there's any help you need in the workshop, just ask me.'

'Thank you for cleaning that space and setting up that light for me. Rafe took me in there the other day and he said that you'd done that. You've been very kind to me, Dylan, and I want you to know I really appreciate it.'

'Just being sociable,' he said.

'No, it's more than that. Even though I've only known you a matter of days, I consider you a friend. You're probably the most honest friend I've ever had. You don't want anything from me, and you care about how I feel.'

Odessa raised one hand and lifted her dark hair. Dylan found it hard to keep his eyes from her long graceful neck. Her skin had already picked up a light olive sheen and her cheeks glowed with colour.

'I like you very much,' she said shyly and looked away. 'If I'm a hassle or interfering with your work, let me know and I'll leave you in peace.'

Dylan reached for her hand and held it gently. 'I like you very much too, Odessa, and I enjoy your company. And I'm honoured to be classed as your friend.'

Her face lit up as she smiled back at him and squeezed his hand. 'And you make the best French toast ever.'

'Ah, wait until you taste my tacos,' he said.

Chapter 25

Odessa

Odessa had been fine when she went to the wharf to see her parents off on the morning boat on Friday. Determined not to cry—she was almost thirty years old, for God's sake—she'd held back the tears when Mummy had clung to her, but they'd spilled over when Dad had held her and said, 'You take care of yourself, chicken.' He hadn't called her that pet name for a long time.

Rafe and Pippa had come down to the boat to see them off, and they walked across to join Odessa at the end of the wharf once her parents were on the boat. Rafe slung an arm around each of their shoulders, and Odessa looked across at Pippa, but her smile was wide and looked genuine. Since she'd offered to vacate her hut and refused to go up and stay with them at the house, she'd sensed that Pippa now held a grudging respect for her.

The boat engines started, and the water churned at the back of the boat as Jiminy, the skipper, cast off the ropes.

'Holy hell,' he cried out.

Pippa stepped forward. 'What's the matter?'

'I had a delivery for one of your guests and I almost forgot. And your mail.' He threw the rope to Rafe and kept the engines idling as he disappeared below. After a moment he reappeared with two large boxes, and a mail satchel. 'Couriered up from Mackay early today. They just caught me before I headed out here. For an Odessa Walker.' He grinned at Odessa, knowing who she was from the wedding.

'Ooh, it's my silversmithing equipment.'

'Go you!' her father called as Jiminy passed the two boxes over to Rafe.

Odessa's smile was wide, and she was surprised when Pippa put an arm around her waist. 'I'm so pleased for you.'

'Thank you, Pippa. I'm pretty happy too.'

Pippa stood close to her as the boat pulled away and Odessa waved to her parents as the boat disappeared around the rocky point at the northern end of the bay.

'Come on. Let's get you set up in your workshop. Rafe, are you right with the boxes?' Pippa linked an arm through hers and a warm glow ran through Odessa, and the sadness at seeing her parents leave dissipated a little.

'Of course, I am.' He stacked the smaller box on top of the large one and followed them along the jetty.

'I know you're moving into the back building later, and we were hoping that you'd come and join us for dinner up at the house,' Pippa asked as they stepped onto the sand.

'I'd love to, thank you.' If Pippa could make an overture, the least Odessa could do was accept.

What a great day, Odessa thought. She was moving into her new room—although as Pippa had warned her, it was basic—her gear had arrived, and Pippa was being extra nice.

Rafe put the boxes on the bench that Dylan had cleared, and he and Pippa headed off to let her unpack.

'Come up at sunset. Champagne on the deck to celebrate your stay,'

Pippa said as they left. 'Rafe's invited Dylan too, we haven't had him up for dinner yet.'

'Sounds good. I'll see you then.'

As much as she was tempted to start unpacking, Odessa knew she would get side-tracked. She had to go and pack up her gear and bring it down here. Even though she had a couple of hours before she had to vacate her room, the housemaids had come over with Jiminy, and it would be good for them if she moved now.

And it meant she'd have more time to unpack, and maybe start work.

Odessa hummed beneath her breath as she headed back to her hut.

***

Dylan

Dylan spent the day working up on the hill above the old house with Danny Riccardo and his team. This week the builders had pegged out the site and had started the excavation for the foundations. He was up there today to plan the layout of the garden. Even though it was staff accommodation, Pippa had requested that the landscaping be in keeping with the rest of the island.

He was looking forward to having dinner up there tonight and running some ideas past Pippa. The morning boat had departed with Odessa's parents a couple of hours ago, and he wondered how she was feeling. He'd told her that he'd be up here today, and he kept an eye out hoping that she'd come up for morning tea.

'Smoko,' Danny called out to him as he walked past and headed down the hill. Dylan wondered what was going on there; Danny Riccardo spent a lot of time over at the day spa hut, "doing the last few jobs", he said every day.

The crew put their tools down, but Dylan decided to keep working in case Odessa came up a bit later.

He shook his head, not knowing where this "friendship" was going, or if he wanted it to go anywhere. He'd watched from the hill as Odessa and Pippa had walked ahead of Rafe who carried some boxes and he was excited for Odessa, knowing it was the equipment she'd been waiting for.

And today was the day that she was moving into his building.

Dylan went down to the staff kitchen at lunchtime and made himself a toasted sandwich. He had to fight the urge to go looking for Odessa. If she'd wanted his company, she would have come up the hill.

Or maybe it was because he was working with others.

Or maybe she was busy?

Dylan pushed the spade into the ground with unnecessary pressure.

Or maybe it was time he stopped thinking about her all day and all night. She needed space, and the last thing she needed to help her recovery was unwanted attention.

Chapter 26

Pippa

As we moved through spring, the south easterly winds died off, and the weather came from the north. The daytime temperature was still comfortable, and the night temperature only got down to the low twenties. Stinger season was here, and I made sure that each guest was briefed about the necessity to wear a stinger suit for swimming and snorkelling while they were on Pentecost Island. The last thing we wanted was a helicopter medivac.

'What are you looking so happy about?' Rafe asked as he came in from the garden carrying some fresh-cut herbs.

'That was Renzo on the phone. With some fabulous news. He met with his mate in Brisbane, the one with the pool company, and he's negotiated a good deal. The guy's had a couple of cancellations and he thinks he can get our pool in by the end of November.'

'Fantastic.' Rafe walked over and kissed me. 'That will make a huge difference to the summer holiday bookings, I'd say.'

'I have to go and tell Eliza to see if we can do it without touching the overdraft and I'll have to meet with Dylan, and I'll have to—' I stopped talking as Rafe pulled me closer.

'Patience, my darling Phillipa. Does it have to be done right this instant? Or can you come and have a wine with me while I get my secret spaghetti sauce cooking?'

I grinned at this man who was teaching me very good habits. 'Yes, I can have a wine, and yes, you are right—as you always seem to be. Yes, I can do all that tomorrow.'

'And you know the best part of the time frame for the pool?'

'I do. It will keep me busy while you start your next book.'

'You do know me well. Now do you want to pour the wine while I chop the herbs?'

'For you, my gorgeous man, I can do that.'

By the time the spaghetti sauce was bubbling on the stove, and Rafe and I had taken time out for a quick shower together, the sun was getting lower in the western sky, and it wasn't long before Dylan and Odessa would arrive.

I stood on the veranda and took a deep breath. Sometimes my happiness frightened me. Warm hands slipped around my waist and Rafe rested his chin on top of my head.

'Okay, babe?'

'Yes, very okay.' I reached down and put my hands over his. 'But I was just thinking how scary it is. I've had too many days that started with intense happiness and ended badly.'

'You still carry a lot of grief from losing your parents and not having any family, don't you, sweetheart?'

'I do. And I know that's why I'm afraid of embracing how I feel when I am happy.'

'I think we need to start our own family.'

I held my breath. 'What? What did you say?'

'I said I think we need to start our own family. I'm not getting any younger, and I'd like to have fun with our children while I'm still fit enough to give piggyback rides and read nursery rhymes.'

I laughed as happiness bubbled up. 'Oh my God, how long have we been married? Six days? And you want to start a family?'

'I do. I don't think we need to focus on it, or worry about it. We can just let nature take its course. What do you think?'

'I guess Tam and Gabe's bub would have a playmate if we did.'

'And we would have a family. A family of our own.' My husband of less than a week turned me around in his arms and lowered his head to kiss me. 'I love you, Pippa and I can't think of anything I'd like more.'

'Not even a bestseller list?'

'Nope. Not even a bestseller list.'

Chapter 27

Dylan

The gods were looking after him this week, Dylan thought as he re-read the letter that had been waiting for him at the office when he'd stopped in on his way down the hill this afternoon. He was going troppo—too much tropical sun. Thinking about Odessa all the time and considering a relationship, more than friendship, after a week, had been totally stupid.

The letter from Siobhan had been a much needed wake-up call.

Dear Dylan. I hope you are well and enjoying your new job. I just wanted to let you know that we have a second son and all is well. Take care. Siobhan.

For God's sake, how many ex-wives—and one who had not even been a satisfactory wife for any time—would write to their ex-husband to tell them that they had had another baby to the guy who had been a better prospect as a husband?

His temper simmered and the last thing he wanted to do was have a social dinner with Rafe and Pippa—and Odessa. For a while Dylan thought about coming up with an excuse and then his better nature took hold.

That would be the wrong thing to do—

And he never did the wrong thing. Nothing in his life had changed, apart from him knowing that his ex now had two children. Thinking about Siobhan, his failed marriage and the subsequent divorce always brought him down.

It was a timely warning to watch his emotions. He would forget about

Siobhan and the new baby, and take it as a wakeup call.

Dylan went back to his room, but there was no sign of Odessa. She must have gone up to the house already. He grabbed his towel and his toiletries bag and tapped carefully on the closed bathroom door.

There was no answer, and when he went in, he flicked the lock over, so he could take a shower without worrying about the door opening.

By the time he'd showered, had a second shave for the day, and put on a pair of dress shorts and a button-up shirt, Dylan was feeling marginally better. He pulled the door of his room closed behind him and headed for the outside door.

As he walked outside, a faint noise from the workshop caught his attention. He paused and listened as the low sounds turned into a full hammering.

Odessa must still be there. Reluctantly he headed back inside and walked to the back of the building where the L-shaped workshop began. Odessa was sitting at the bench, the only light was the desk lamp he had placed there for her. A halo of light silhouetted her, and as he stood there, she lifted a piece of silver up to the light.

She twirled it slowly, and when she took a deep shuddering breath, Dylan knew he had to let her know he was there.

'Odessa?' he said quietly.

She turned slowly, still holding the piece of silver. As she faced him, he could see the silver was shaped into a perfect H-shape.

'Hello, Dylan.' Her voice was thick, and tears were running down her face.

He took a step back, knowing that he was intruding on a private moment.

'I'm just about to go up to Pippa and Rafe's. Are you still going up for dinner?'

Her eyes widened and she rubbed the back of her hand on her cheeks. 'I lost track of the time.'

'Would you like me to wait for you?'

When she shook her head, he was a little disappointed, yet also relieved. 'Okay, I'll head on up, and let them know you'll be up soon.'

Dylan turned away, and he knew she'd forgotten he was there before he'd even reached the door.

***

Odessa

It was another hour before Odessa was satisfied with the piece she had created for Vivian. All the knowledge that she had learned in the silversmithing course came back to her as she sawed and filed, then soldered and buffed the shape.

Dylan had come in when she had first finished the soldering, but she had been so emotional when she saw the H, she had barely registered his presence.

He was a kind and gentle man, but she wasn't ready for a romance. She had a lot to sort out before she'd get to that. That was the sensible way to do things anyway.

After a quick wash and a change of clothes, she brushed her hair, and left it loose, before walking up the hill to Rafe's—and Pippa's—house.

The fragrant aroma of tomato and garlic reached her as she climbed the last steps. Rafe and Pippa, and Dylan were sitting outside watching the sunset.

As Odessa opened the gate, the last of the sun slipped below the horizon, sending a shimmering gold to touch the clouds above. It was one of the most beautiful sunsets she'd ever seen, and serenity filled her.

Dylan and Rafe both stood as she approached the table where the three of them were sitting. Rafe took her hand and kissed her cheek. 'Welcome to our home, Odessa.'

Pippa raised her glass and greeted her. 'Welcome.'

Dylan sat back down without speaking.

It was a strange night. Despite the fact that everyone seemed preoccupied, and conversation was desultory, Odessa felt at ease. Finishing the piece for Vivian in one afternoon and knowing that she could do it had given her a huge boost.

And a purpose.

The meal was delicious, and both she and Dylan covered yawns as Rafe brought coffee out.

'Sorry,' Odessa said. 'It's been a big day. I hope you don't mind but as soon as I finish my coffee, I'm going to go back down.'

'I'll walk down with you.' Dylan smiled for the first time that night. 'We're going to the same place.'

'That's fine,' Pippa said. 'I think we're all tired. tonight. The week has caught up with me, I know that.'

Rafe and Pippa both kissed Odessa goodnight as she and Dylan left, and Odessa felt as though she had been accepted . . . finally.

Epilogue

Odessa had done a lot of thinking this afternoon and if it suited Rafe and Pippa, she decided she would like to stay on the island for a longer time.

'Penny for your thoughts?' Dylan asked when they reached the jetty, and Odessa realised they had not spoken a word since they had said goodbye to Rafe and Pippa.

'I'm sorry. I was too quiet,' she said. 'That was rude of me.'

'In that case I was rude too as I was quiet too. We all seemed to be lost in our thoughts,' Dylan replied, and Odessa thought he sounded sad. He was right. No one had been themselves tonight. Pippa and Rafe had seemed to be in their own little world too.

'You have something on your mind?' she asked.

'Yeah, a couple of things.'

She stopped and took his hand. 'A problem shared and all that? If you want to talk, I'm a good listener.' She lightened her words with a chuckle. 'As long as you promise not to cry all over my shoulder.'

He smiled again. 'You've got enough on your plate without listening to my minor woes.'

'I'm feeling good, Dylan. It's all upwards from here for me now, so try me. You were a sounding board for me, so the least I can do is reciprocate.'

'Thank you.' Gentle hands touched her shoulders. 'I got a letter today from my ex-wife.'

'I didn't know you'd been married,' she said.

'My wife left me for my best mate. They've just had their second baby, and foolishly I let it bother me. And that was stupid. I wasn't unhappy for long when we got divorced, so I need to move on.'

'As long as you can talk about your feelings and understand them, that's a good thing. God, I'm sounding like my psychologist. But you know what? I think I finally got there today. Making that piece of jewellery for Hannah's grandmother was a defining moment for me. I've decided I'd like to stay on Pentecost Island for at least six months. If it's okay with Pippa and Rafe, that is. I'm going to get a portfolio together, and I'm going to attempt a career as a silversmith.' She turned her face up to his and realised how close he was. A pleasant warmth ran down her back, and Odessa reached her hand up to touch Dylan's face. 'You said woes. As in more than one. What were the others?'

'There was only one other.' He cupped his palm over her hand and held it against his face.

'I'm going to be honest with you, Odessa. I've only known you for a week, but the attraction I feel for you is like nothing I've ever experienced before. I've fought it, and I decided I was going to avoid you. But you know what? I can't. I sat and watched you at Rafe and Pippa's tonight. And I loved watching you. I love being with you.'

'Well, I'm going to be here for a while, so maybe we could explore that more? How would that be?' As she spoke, she'd moved closer to him, and his breath fanned her face as he held her eyes with his.

'I think that would be a very good idea.' His lips were millimetres away from hers and Odessa closed them as he moved closer until their lips were touching. 'But we'll go slow. How does that sound?' His words vibrated against her lips.

'I think that sounds very suitable.'

All was quiet for a long time as Dylan held her close. His warm lips explored hers and his hands caressed her bare back.

Reluctantly, she pulled away as she heard a boat motor getting closer and louder.

They stood together in the dark, and there was just enough new moon to see the silhouette of a rubber tender as the vessel scraped on the shingly sand. A figure jumped out and ran up the beach as the boat left the beach and roared off into the night.

'That was strange,' Dylan said.

'It was, and you know what, I could have sworn that that was Sienna who ran up the beach.'

Dylan held her hand as they crossed the sand. As they approached the small glade at the top of the beach path, the hoarse sound of sobs reached them, and then faded. They paused and looked at each other as they caught a glimpse of a figure beneath the light of the veranda of the old house.

'It is Sienna,' Odessa said. 'I recognised the white jacket she wears in the spa.'

She stood on her toes and brushed her lips across Dylan's. 'You go back to your room, and I'll go and see what's wrong.'

'Try not to be too long. I'd like to talk some more.'

'I'll see you soon.' Odessa walked up the steps of the house as Dylan headed around the side. As she stepped inside, a light came on in the kitchen where Dylan had cooked her breakfast last weekend.

She moved quietly through the loungeroom and paused at the kitchen door. Odessa's eyes widened and a gasp escaped her lips.

Sienna was sitting at the table, her head in her hands as she cried soundlessly. Her white jacket was covered in blood.

***

Do you want to know what trouble Sienna has got herself into?

Sienna quickly fits into the friendship group on the island but holds her shameful secret close to her heart. When she falls in love with builder, Danny Riccardo, she knows she cannot succumb to her feelings. Longing to be loved, Sienna finds herself alone for a week with the one man she cannot afford to love..

Click on the link below to pre-order.

https://www.annieseaton.net/store.html
If you are enjoying the Pentecost Island series, come and meet the McDougal siblings at Second Chance Bay. A special offer... all four stories are available in print individually from Annie's store

https://www.annieseaton.net/store.html

Other Books

All available in print from: https://www.annieseaton.net/store.html

Whitsunday Dawn
Undara

Coming soon: Osprey Reef (2021)

Porter Sisters Series

Kakadu Sunset

Daintree

Diamond Sky

Hidden Valley (2021)

Pentecost Island Series (2020)

Pippa

Eliza

Nell

Tamsin

Evie

Cherry

Odessa

Sienna

Tess

Isla

Bondi Beach Love Series

Beach House

Beach Music

Beach Walk

Beach Dreams

The House on the Hill

Second Chance Bay Series

Her Outback Playboy

Her Outback Protector

Her Outback Haven

Her Outback Paradise

Love Across Time Series

Come Back to Me

Follow Me

Finding Home (November 2020)

The Threads that Bind (2021)

Others

The Trouble with Paradise

Deadly Secrets

Adventures in Time

Silver Valley Witch

The Emerald Necklace

Worth the Wait

Ten Days in Paradise

Acknowledgements

A special thank you to my wonderful editor and critique partner, Susanne Bellamy, and my eagle-eyed proof-readers, Roby Aiken, Nicki Edwards, Anna Welch and Kristen Woolgar.

About the Author

Finalist for the NZ KORU award 2018 and 2020.

Winner ...Best Established Author of the Year 2017 AUSROM

Long listed for the Sisters in Crime Davitt Awards 2016, 2017, 2018, 2019

Finalist in Book of the Year, Long Romance, RWA Ruby awards 2016

Winner ...Best Established Author of the Year 2015 AUSROM

Winner ...Author of the Year 2014 AUSROM

Best Established Author, Ausrom Readers' Choice 2017

Book of the Year (Whitsunday Dawn) Ausrom Readers' Choice Awards 2018

Annie lives in Australia, on the beautiful north coast of New South

Wales. She sits in her writing chair and looks out over the tranquil Pacific Ocean. She has fulfilled her lifelong dream of becoming an author and is producing books at a prolific rate.

She writes contemporary romance and loves telling the stories that always have a happily Ever after. She lives with her very own hero of many years and they share their home with Toby, the naughtiest dog in the universe, and Barney, the rag doll kitten, who hides when the grandchildren come to visit.

Stay up to date with her latest releases at her website: http://www.annieseaton.net